THE TELLTALE TART

THE TELLTALE TART

PETER DUNCAN

CUTTING EDGE

ISBN-13: 978-1-957868-34-9

Published by
Cutting Edge Books
PO Box 8212
Calabasas, CA 91372
www.cuttingedgebooks.com

CHAPTER ONE

'd had some ugly surprises in my thirty-one years but usually they had come one at a time. My second day on Spanish Point island, though, they started coming in bunches. One surprise was finding out that *Chic* magazine hadn't sent me down just to shoot pictures of John Hope Hamilton, his private island, and Oakhurst, his ancestral estate. What I had really been sent down for could wind up in murder. Maybe, mine.

Another ugly surprise was finding out the loathsome truth about Laura Ames, the good-looking blonde staff writer I had been sent down with. She wasn't at all what I had been promised she would be. Instead, she was a nice girl.

The ugliest surprise of all, though, was finding out that nothing but flounders, seals and grunions should try mating in a high surf. It's too hard on humans.

I found that out with the help of Cuba—Hecuba—Paxton. She was John Hamilton's secretary, but—as sexy as she was—he must have done his dictating to her either wearing blinkers or hollering to her over a transom. She had shiny black hair, big dark eyes, a beautiful Spanish-type face and a smile so evil and suggestive that, if it had been on a man, the police would have pulled all his teeth.

The rest of her was even more disturbing. She was tall and slender but still voluptuous, if you know what I mean, and she could throw that voluptuousness around in such a way that she looked like she had been built with hinges instead of bones.

But she didn't have the brains to match all that. At least I didn't think so at the time. It seemed that she was trying to make both Laura and Hamilton jealous and thought that she could use me to do it. Even though I was six feet, three inches tall and weighed over two hundred pounds, she thought she could flaunt her charms at me in any sort of way and, because I was such a nice, friendly, easy-going sort of fellow and such a gentleman, she wouldn't have to worry about my making her pay off.

Ordinarily, she would have been right, but this time, due to certain circumstances beyond my control, she was wrong. So, the morning of that second day, she walked right into her own trap.

It was around nine o'clock and Laura and Hamilton had gone off on a tour of the island right after breakfast. That left me wandering around the downstairs of the huge old twenty-room mansion debating where to set up my cameras and wondering just what sort of mess I had gotten into this time. Nothing I had run into during my eighteen hours on the island had been what I expected.

Finally, I decided to set up in the Green Parlor, as they called it, but then Cuba strolled in. She had a beachrobe cloaked over her shoulders and, underneath, a white, skirtless, one-piece bathing suit that fit her like a tattoo.

"Pete, sugar," she said, "wouldn't you like to take Cuba to the beach?"

Girls who refer to themselves in the third person usually remind me of a cheap ventriloquist act, but I didn't too much mind Cuba's doing it. She lapsed into it only when she was on the make and, besides, no matter what person she talked in, that soft, velvety voice still sounded like she had just sprayed her throat with love potions.

So I told her I was sorry. I appreciated the invitation, but I had forgotten to bring my life preserver and ear plugs along. She did just about what I figured she would do: strolled over, started twisting a button on my shirt like she was cranking up a motor, smiled up at me and said, "We don't have to go swimming, silly. We can play games."

"What kind of games?" I asked.

"Any kind you want to play, sugar."

"You got a beach ball?"

"No, but I've got something that's a lot more fun. And it's got lots more bounce to it."

With that, I figured that she had committed herself so far that even an all-woman jury wouldn't blame me for what I was going to do. I went up and got into my bathing trunks, rolled up some beach accessories in a towel and fifteen minutes later we were in Hamilton's jeep headed for Cuba's favorite spot.

The island was about two miles off the mainland, some six miles long and three across at the widest point. As it had been owned by the Hamiltons for about two hundred years, and occupied exclusively by them and their servants, I didn't have to worry about traffic on the two little sandy ruts that were supposed to be a road. All I had to worry about was running over bears, alligators, wildcats, deer, racoons, turkeys and maybe Hansel and Gretel.

That's how wild it was. Once you got a hundred yards or so from the house you ran into a jungle of live oaks, cypress, wild magnolia, palmettos, vines, undergrowth, black water ponds, tidal creeks and sinkholes. A quarter of a mile of it could be quite pretty but then the dankness and gloom started seeping into your soul. Pretty soon you began to feel like a mole in a big, dark green tunnel lined with Spanish moss.

The cheeriest sight we saw the whole trip was the family cemetery, its headstones making it look like a white asparagus patch. It was in a clearing, canopied by oaks, on the banks of a tidal creek.

Cuba said there were five or six generations of Hamiltons buried there, all in cypress coffins made from island trees. It was a family tradition, and Hamilton and Miss Maude, his old maid sister, already had their coffins made up and stored in the loft over the horse barn out back of the house. I told her that was real interesting but that if she didn't keep her hand off my knee while I was driving, *we* might wind up being buried in them instead.

Finally, the road twisted out of the jungle and deposited us at a spot so wild, so lonely, so beautiful that it looked like one of those tropical island travel ads. In living color. The dark green of the jungle behind us; above us, a blue sky; before us, a shining white beach bordered on one side by a spidery windrow of silvery drift, on the other by great, sparkling green breakers. And, except for some gulls wheeling and crying overhead and a fishing boat about three miles out, we had it all to ourselves.

It was such a relief from that jungle, such a feast for the eyes and soul that I forgot about Cuba—for maybe ten seconds. She got pouty. "Well, aren't you going to thank Cuba for bringing you to such a pretty place? And getting you out of that gloomy old house?"

I thanked her. I pulled her to me and kissed her. Then she put her arms around my neck and kissed me. When she got through I wanted to yank her mouth open and see whether she had a tongue in it or an electric eel.

But it was just what I needed to harden my heart to the task at hand. I piled out of the jeep and started blowing up an air mattress that I had brought down to the island thinking that Laura and I might be needing it.

Cuba played it innocent. She acted like she thought I was going to use it for a raft. She took off her robe—which made me gasp so that I sucked half the air back out of the mattress—and then she spread out her big beach towel and sat down on it and watched me.

Finally, I got it blown up and strolled over and laid it down in front of her. I figured that after all the torture she had put me through and all the things she had said, I was entitled to skip the preliminaries and get on with the main bout.

"Cuba," I said, "we are going to play a game called the Romans and the Sabines. It's real simple, *if* you follow the rules. All you've got to do is get up, spread your beach towel on this air mattress and then take off your bathing suit."

I expected her to do what her type usually did: get outraged, jump to her feet and, in a loud, virtuous voice, demand to know what sort of girl I thought she was. Instead, she just looked amused.

"But suppose Cuba doesn't want to take her suit off?"

"Well, that's when the game gets complicated," I said. "I take it off for you."

She kept smiling. "But why do you want to play a game like that, sugar?" I knew that her stalling and acting so cool must be leading up to some fiendish sort of trick, so I decided to take a couple of minutes off and explain to her what a desperate man she was dealing with and why her fiendish trick wasn't going to work.

"All right," I said. "I'll tell you why I want to play this game. Then, you won't object so much when we go ahead and play it anyway."

I couldn't keep my voice from getting a little grim but she didn't seem to mind. She patted the towel and said, "Well, you sit right down here and tell Cuba all about it."

I did just that. I sat down and proceeded to tell her the tragic story of how I had happened to come to Spanish Point and how she was going to ease my sorrow.

It had all started with the Korean War and a monster named Ben Ponza. He was the Executive Director of Brandt Publications, an outfit with about twelve magazines that ranged all the way from *Probe,* a news magazine, down to *Pursuit,* a detective magazine.

Well, when Ben decided to play at being a war correspondent and went to Korea, where I already was, I was relieved of my job as platoon leader and assigned to chauffeur him around and see that he didn't get himself killed. I saved his life about eight times, mostly by tucking him under my arm and running back to the jeep. Then, when he was heading back to the States, he wanted to know if there wasn't something he could do for me. I told him there was.

I said that I was planning on doing some free-lance photography when I got out, and if any of his magazines had pictures they wanted taken down in my part of the country, I would certainly appreciate the business.

He told me I could count on it, and unfortunately, he was a man of his word. Every time one of his magazines wanted some pictures that might require a fight to take, I got the assignment. I took some pictures at a cock-fight—strictly against the law, cock-fighting is—and, when the promoter and his boys found out what I was doing, I wound up doing more fighting than all them roosters put together.

Then I had hid out in some wet, cold woods for three days and three nights taking pictures of some moonshiners in action. Once, when I thought they had left the still unguarded, I sneaked down to run off a batch to combat the pneumonia I was developing and they caught me. I had to fight my way out of that, too.

All the time there were assignments like that, and I would come back from them with more lumps than a bottle of buttermilk. Finally, when I got a pick handle broken over my head covering a coal strike in east Kentucky, I wrote Ben a letter. I told him that I appreciated all he had done for me but I was getting too full of years and scar tissue to let him do it any longer.

I wound up by saying that unless he could send me on a nice, quiet, lush assignment with some real pretty, *affectionate* lady writer, I was through working for him. Three days later I got an airmail special delivery letter. He said that his editors had never said a word to him about my terrible trials and tribulations and he was horrified. But he was going to make it up to me.

He said he was having his women's magazine, *Chic,* send me down for a week to a beautiful island named Spanish Point with a beautiful staff writer named Laura Ames. The owner of this island, he said, was none other than John Hope Hamilton, the distinguished novelist. Not only was he a great writer, he was also a great gentleman. Anyone fortunate enough to visit his beautiful old ancestral home, Oakhurst, would long remember his fabulous hospitality, as well as that of his charming sister, Maude.

But most of all, he said, I would enjoy the favors of the beauteous Laura. He had it on good authority that the only thing she didn't know about making love was when to stop.

Naturally, I jumped at the assignment. And not because I was a lecher. I was just human and was thinking of the welfare of my family and my home town of Stanton. My mother is a big church-woman; Aunt Nora, who is going to leave me all her money, is on the board of a home for unwed mothers; my father is the county judge and just itching to get me up before him on some charge so that he can get even with me for becoming a photographer instead of a lawyer.

What with a family like that and Stanton being a fairly small place, I had always made it a point to get my serious recreation when I was out of town on assignments. But on my last three assignments I had been too busy fighting to do anything else and it had left me so starved for affection, etc., that I was about to commit civic incest and turn on the girls in my own home town.

So, it wasn't any wonder that Ben's letter set me wild. I spent the two weeks prior to my departure dreaming about Laura and me under the magnolias, on the veranda, in the summerhouse, on the beach, and so forth. By the time I met her at Queensport, the jumping-off place to Spanish Point, I had myself convinced that the job wasn't going to be anything but a seven-day love feast.

Then the dream started falling apart. Laura was as pretty as Ben had said, but I got the feeling right away that somebody had given him some bum dope about her hobbies.

As for Spanish Point, nobody but Tarzan would call it a semi-tropical paradise. Oakhurst, the old mansion, looked like *Gone With the Wind* from the outside but inside it was more like the House of Usher. Except for the plumbing, the heating, and the lights, not a thing had been changed for a hundred years, outside of the sheets.

The servant situation wasn't any better. I had been expecting a lot of nice, friendly, old family retainers but instead there was just a white couple named Jago and Mattie. Jago was even bigger than I was and looked like a landlocked pirate. Mattie looked just as mean and when she got dolled up in her white uniform she could pass for the head nurse in an abortion mill.

As for the "fabulously hospitable" Hamilton, he had been all of that to Laura but he had made it pretty plain that I was more a member of the working press than a guest. Which was all right, but his overtones of lechery and arrogance gave me the uneasy feeling that Ben Ponza had sent us down for some reason other than to glorify him in picture and print.

And Cuba was a puzzle, too. Why was such a wild, gorgeous creature wasting her time and talents on a snob like Hamilton and a place like Spanish Point?

Miss Maude, Hamilton's old maid sister was the only one who had come anywhere close to fitting Ben's advance notice. She *was* charming. She was a jolly, dumpy little thing of sixty or so with dyed reddish blonde hair, puffy blue eyes—from too much whiskey I figured—and had a way of blurting out the first thing that came to mind. One of the clubwoman types you see in the cartoons. But as much as I liked her, she was still about thirty years older than I had expected. I had even been figuring on having a little fun with her, too.

Laura, though, was the one who really killed the dream. Even after figuring that Ben was wrong about her, I had kept hoping. The set-up was so perfect. Miss Maude, bless her old heart, had given us adjoining rooms, sharing the same bathroom.

So I had spent the first evening trying to keep away from Cuba. When she and Miss Maude and I played some sort of rummy game after dinner, she kept patting my knee, rubbing her leg against mine, and when she would stand behind me and kibitz, she would drape her charms around my neck and jiggle.

She knew she was running me crazy but because I didn't want to mess up my chances with Laura, I just ignored her. Then, at bedtime, I slipped into my new silk pajamas, laid out the fancy red nightgown I had brought down for Laura, sneaked into the bathroom and rapped gently on her bedroom door.

I thought I looked real nice and gentlemanly in a seductive sort of way but she must have thought I looked like a plain sex maniac, because she slammed the door on my head.

Now, that was my story and, in effect, it was what I told Cuba. Only I added a few more colorful details about how she had tormented me and I apologized for seeming to have preferred Laura's charms to hers. She ignored that part of it, ignored my wondering about her being on the island, and smiled sympathetically.

"Oh, that is a sad story, sugar," she said. "Cuba feels so sorry for you."

"I thought you would," I said. "And, now, you understand why I'm making you play that game."

The little smile stayed on her face, and very casually, she got to her feet. I knew the crisis was at hand. I stood up, too, and reminded her of what she had said before we left the house. The smile turned into a mocking grin.

"But you just said that you were going to *make* Cuba play the game. Sugar, you don't really think you're man enough to *make* Cuba do anything, do you?"

Right then I knew her for what she was: one of those damn cave-woman types. They want you to have it but they don't want to give it to you, they want you to *take* it. Fight for it. They get some sort of primitive, masochistic thrill out of being forced to give it up. I'd had a girl like that in college. She finally kicked the inside of my old Studebaker clean apart.

"Cuba," I said, sweetly, "take the suit off."

She confirmed my diagnosis. Her eyes started shining, she planted her hands on her hips, threw her chest out and smirked:

"*Make* me!"

I grabbed for her and one of her hands flew up. I hadn't noticed that it had sand in it. It splattered in my face and she raced, laughing, across the beach towards the breakers. It was a typical cave-woman trick. That college girl had once chewed up my right ear so bad, that for a month it looked like a teething ring.

By the time I got the sand out of my eyes, Cuba was bobbing out through the breakers. She turned around, still laughing, saw me coming, screamed and started swimming out to sea. It was like a bone having to chase a dog. She let me catch her about twenty yards out beyond the breakers. First, I had her by the foot, then around the waist and then around the heart.

She let out another of her girlish screams and started fighting like she wanted to get loose. I started peeling off her suit. When she came out of it, she made Venus, coming naked out of that seashell look like an old man taking off an overcoat.

She really screamed then but I calmly looped the straps around my neck and let the suit dangle down my back. Then I got out of my trunks. I ran my arm through one leg and pushed the whole business up to my shoulder. She could have swum off any time but she just kept treading water, flaunting her ivory and ebony charms and saying, "Damn, you, Pete Farrell, if you touch me I'll …"

I reached out, grabbed her and pulled her to me. Her breasts pressed against my chest, then the rest of her. I gasped and locked my arms around her waist and pulled her even closer. She started having trouble with her own breathing, too, but she tried to hide it. She put her arms around my neck, rested her chin on my shoulder and murmured, "Sugar, you can lead Cuba to water but you still can't make her. You'll just drive yourself crazy."

And that was just what I proceeded to do. It was like trying to shake hands on a pogo stick. I could stand up, the water was just halfway up my chest, but the waves kept wafting me shoreward and that damn gorgeous Cuba, despite all my efforts to hold on to her, kept slithering up and down me. One second I'd be looking her in the eye, the next second I'd be looking her in the chest.

"Help me!" I whined. "You're worse than a damn seal."

That made her mad because she was beginning to take a real interest in the proceedings, too.

"I'm trying to help you," she snapped. "Get in closer." I misunderstood her and tried to do what I thought she wanted but my foot slipped and we both went under "Not closer to *me*, you stupid sonofabitch!" she spluttered. "Closer to the shore where it's shallower!"

That was the best and worst idea of the day. I pulled her to me again and slowly started backing into shallower water. Then, all in one glorious moment, I shuddered and gasped, she shuddered and gasped, I grabbed her tighter, she grabbed me tighter and then I went out of my mind.

I mean I really did. One second I was having these ecstatic fits and Cuba was kissing me and having fits right back and then the next thing I knew she was fighting to get loose and screaming about being in the breakers. I didn't give a damn about breakers or anything else, but then, what must have been the biggest wave to hit that shore in years caught us up in it.

It was like going over Niagara Falls in a love-seat. The whole world turned green and wet but, at first, I didn't mind because the wave just tumbled us over and over and I thought to myself, "Now, man, this is really living!" But then we hit bottom and another wave caught us and we parted. Cuba started bumping along on my head, I started bumping along on my stomach and then I was shooting through rocks, shell and gravel at about ninety miles an hour.

The next thing I knew, I was lying on my face about fifteen feet up on the beach and Cuba was standing over me raising hell. "You even lost the suits! You stupid, stupid, *stupid* sonofabitch!"

I just lay there and felt around. Sure enough, that wave had tumbled me loose from the suits. But even with my stomach scraped just about raw and my game interrupted, too, I felt right good. Though I hadn't accomplished my mission, there wasn't any doubt but that I was going to. I rolled over and looked up at Cuba. She struck a September Morn pose and glared down at me. "*Get* my suit!"

I laughed and told her to stop worrying, the suits would wash in. "Let's go back and finish that game. I think we've got the hang of it, now."

She looked like she wanted to kill me but then she couldn't help laughing. "To hell with you, Davy Jones. You find those suits. I'm going to get my robe."

"I'll just take it right back off!"

"Oh, you think so?" she said, giving me that mocking smile again.

"And you'll help me," I said. "Just like you helped me when I took that suit off."

The smile got bigger and, like a fool, I thought it just meant that she was admitting the truth. She turned and started walking towards the jeep and I watched her every step of the way, She had a bottom so gorgeous, it would make a harvest moon look like a tiddly wink. I could hardly wait. I was on the verge of my finest hour.

When she started putting on the robe, I got up and walked along the beach looking for the suits. I didn't want anything distracting her mind from the game. I must have poked along a couple of minutes, studying the waves and dreaming my mad dreams. Then suddenly it occurred to me that it was taking her a mighty long time to get back with that robe. And, at the very same time, over the roar of the waves, I heard another roar. I turned around, looked back, and panicked.

She had the jeep turned around and was getting ready to take off. I raced across the beach pleading and cursing: "Cuba, baby, wait! ... Honey, you don't have to play that game ... Sugarfoots, you wouldn't leave old Pete naked ... You sleazy bitch, come back here!"

I got within about twenty yards of her and she laughed, waved, hollered something and the jeep roared off down the road through the jungle. I raced after it, grabbed hold of the spare tire and was just about to jump aboard when she hit a mud puddle. It was like dropping a depth bomb in a pig pen. This sheet of black slop shot up higher than my head. It blinded me, soaked me and shook me loose from the jeep.

I limped back to where the jeep had been parked, looking like the tar-baby's daddy. I wanted to get my towel but she had taken everything: my towel, her towel, the mattress, even my cigarettes. Maybe she had gotten more out of the game than I had; maybe, being the fiendish bitch she was, she just couldn't stand a man having the upper hand too long.

Whatever it was, I didn't have any illusions about her coming back. She would go to the house, make certain that everybody knew she didn't have a suit on under the robe and, when asked what had happened to that nice, friendly, gentlemanly boy she had fared forth with, she would smile the smile of the Sabine women and let them guess.

Then Laura and Hamilton would come after me. I wouldn't be wearing anything but horsefly bites and a stupid grin. That, coupled with Cuba's condition, would add up to the perfect case of sea-going rape. Attempted rape, at least, which would make me look even more stupid.

About a half hour later, I was pacing up and down the beach, cussing, slapping at flies and waving a big palm branch I had found washed up. I was trying to hail the fishing boat we'd seen when we first drove up. It had moved in a lot closer and now was running parallel to the beach in my direction. Finally, it hove to about a hundred yards out. I took a last look down the road for the jeep, fought my way out through the breakers and started swimming.

The boat was a beat-up little trawler named the "Eleanor T." Standing at the rail watching me were three fellows about my age—one great big one, one middle-sized one of about a hundred and ninety pounds and one short one about a yard across. They were all black-headed, tattooed, real sunburned and stripped to the waist. To tell the truth, they looked like a cargo of apes but they had good hearts. I could tell that by the way they were grinning at me.

When I swam alongside, they said they had been watching me through the glasses and they just bet I wanted to borrow some britches. I told them that I sure did. The biggest one asked me if I was a friend of John Hamilton's and when I said I was, their grins got bigger. They reached down and helped me aboard. As soon as my feet hit the deck, I knew I had been tricked again.

Their grins turned to leers and the middle one looked me over like it was hog-killing time and said, "Well, well, well! Ain't he pretty!" The big one said, "Just like one of them Greek gods, ain't he?" Then he said that maybe they could arrange to have me put in a cell with a window in it so the women in Queensport could see me.

The stocky one explained that. He said they were putting me under citizen's arrest and taking me to the Queensport jail for indecent exposure, rape, and corrupting the morals of Christian fishermen. That last charge got a big laugh from the other two but I felt like weeping. After what Cuba had done to me, I just wasn't in the mood for any more jokes. I tried explaining that to them but the big one drowned me out.

"This ain't no joke!" he said. "Every time one of us po' crackers sets a foot on that island to do a little hunting or picnicking or anything, yo' friend Hamilton tries throwing us in jail. We gonna put yo' big naked butt in jail and show him what it's like."

That didn't make me as mad as it did sad. It gave me the feeling that, despite the dirty trick they were trying to play on me, they weren't really bad fellows. John Hamilton, evidently had been acting so high and mighty and making folks so mad that they would strike back at him any way they could.

But, when I tried explaining that I wasn't really a friend of his, they just laughed and claimed I was trying to crawfish out of it. I knew then that I would either have to fight or go to jail. I got my back to the wheel so they couldn't get at me from behind and told them to come on.

"Bachelors first!" I said. "I hate to hit the ones with children."

The big one lunged at me and let go with an old roundhouse right that never would have landed if I hadn't been keeping my eye on the other two. It caught me on the cheek and the whole side of my face went numb. I didn't mind, though, because I could see that the other two thought he could handle me by himself.

He swung the right again, I stepped inside it and hit him in the stomach. He gave a big grunt, doubled over and I straightened him up. He lit on his back about six feet out and lay there. I rubbed my cheek, looked at the other two and asked them real nicely to let's be friends.

"If I have to fight the two of you together," I said, "I'll have to fight dirty and that can *really* be painful."

They stared down at the big one who still looked like he was lying in state, and then the stocky one said, "You really ain't any friend of Hamilton's, are you?"

I explained to them that I was just on the island shooting pictures and I didn't like Hamilton any better than they did. That made them a whole lot happier. The stocky one got a bucket of sea water and sloshed it on the big one. When he came around and got his eyes back in focus, they told him it didn't hurt as much as he thought it did: I was a friend of theirs not Hamilton's.

He got to his feet, shook my hand, introduced himself and the others, and asked them what the hell they meant letting company stand around naked. They were the Stokes brothers: Harney, the big one, Charlie, the middle one, and Puss.

Puss opened some beer and Charlie rummaged around in a locker, while I tried to get Harney to tell me why they hated John Hamilton. "It's more than just trespassing on his island," I said. You could see it in their eyes. They *really* hated Gentleman John. But Harney was like a lot of people who are close-mouthed around strangers. They'll tell you a man is a no-good bastard but they won't tell you why.

Those were Harney's sentiments. He just called Hamilton a bunch of dirty names and said there wasn't anybody in Queens county, except Miss Maude, who wouldn't like to see him dead.

"And it might'n be too long 'fore he winds up that way neither."

"Then there *is* something besides trespassing?" I said. "You don't kill a man just for …"

"You'll hear about it some day," he said. "Give him another beer, Puss."

He really had me curious, then, and uneasy, too, but before I could get anything else out of him, Charlie held up a red bathing suit and asked me if I could use it. That took my mind completely off Hamilton. The bathing suit looked like it would fit but there was just one little thing wrong with it: it was a woman's suit. It had a ruffled skirt, fluff around the edges and straps that tied around the neck.

"Sis left it on here last Sunday," Harney said. "We took the family on a picnic."

Well, you can't say to a man, "Godalmighty, just how big a sister you got?" And, as they didn't seem to see anything funny in it, I acted like I didn't either and put it on. She must have been the biggest woman in the state because, when I let the straps all the way out, it fit pretty good. I felt like a damn fool but they just commented that they knew Sis wouldn't mind. Then, Harney said that they would run me down the beach a couple of miles where there was a road that wasn't but about a half mile back to the house.

So, we got under way. It was about a fifteen-minute run, not long enough for me to find out any more about Hamilton. Instead they talked about the northeaster that was blowing in. The general consensus was that my luck was on an ebb tide. First, that girl had done me the way she did; now, I was going to be cooped up in that old house for three days, maybe, in a storm. It was full of ghosts, they said. I told them that might change my luck, I sure as hell wasn't doing any good with live girls.

Then, Harney pointed towards the beach at a road coming out of the woods. "There she is," he said, cutting the engine. I shook hands all around and told them I never would forget what they'd done for me. Then I asked where I could drop their sister's suit. They said I could leave it at the Queensport dock, where they kept their boat.

"Well, can't I do something to repay you?" I said. "What about taking a nice picture of your boat when I come back over? I'll do it in color and you can frame it."

Puss started to say something that I didn't think had anything to do with the picture, but Harney drowned him out and said I didn't owe them a thing. It was their pleasure helping somebody who didn't like Hamilton any better than they did.

So, I told them good-bye again and went over the side. I'd swum maybe twenty yards when I heard one of them hollering at me. I stopped, started treading water and looked back.

"Farrell," Puss hollered, "you can do us a favor. Ask Hamilton what *really* happened to Mary Belle Clayton."

With that Harney and Charlie told him to shut up. I started to swim back to the boat but Harney was getting under way. "What about Mary Belle?" I hollered.

"Never mind!" Harney hollered back.

Puss was fighting Charlie off. Charlie was trying to slap his hand over his mouth. "Find out from Miss Maude, then," Puss yelled. "Mary Belle Clayton!"

With that they took off, both Charlie and Harley giving Puss hell. I turned and started swimming for the beach. Even in that girl's bathing suit I felt better. I didn't know who Mary Belle Clayton was but I had the feeling that when I found out I would know why I had *really* been sent down to Spanish Point.

CHAPTER TWO

The road up from the beach wasn't quite as dismal as the Little Red Riding Hood route that Cuba and I had taken, and after about fifteen minutes of bare-footing it through the cool, gray sand, I could see old Oakhurst at the end of the tunnel of live oaks I was in.

Joshua Hamilton had built the place back in the early 1800's with rice and indigo money. It was a huge, weathered brick affair with white trim, dark green shutters and eight big fat white columns out front. Across the second floor there was a big porch, or gallery, as Hamilton insisted on calling it. The four bedrooms all had French doors that opened on to it so that you could sit out on hot summer nights in the old rocking chairs and catch the ocean breeze. If the breeze was from the marsh, you probably used the chairs to fight off mosquitoes.

Seen in a picture, shot full view, the house would probably look right pretty. But in person, with the tall, dark windows peering out between the columns like big, black eyes, and being ringed around by a regular forest of huge, old, moss-draped oaks, it had the melancholy air of an old lady who has known happy times in days long gone and now is sorry she didn't go with 'em.

Out front there was a circular, shell driveway that coiled around about eight of the oaks like a big white snake. As I neared it from the beach side, I heard the sound of laughter. I ducked behind a bush because I wasn't about to let anybody see me in that bathing suit. Looking toward the house through the trees, I saw Cuba and Miss Maude sitting out on the front porch. Cuba had changed into a white dress, and the way she had Miss Maude laughing, she could have been telling her what had happened on the beach. At least part of it.

I tried to catch what she was saying but then I heard a car off to my right. It swung into the driveway from the road that Cuba and I had taken. It was Hamilton's blue station wagon. He was at the wheel and Laura was with him. They went around to the right, pulled up in front of the house and got out.

As usual, he was playing the country squire. He had on one of those sloppy, tweed hats, a hacking jacket, riding pants and even though he hadn't been near a horse all morning, he was carrying a riding crop.

But I had to admit that he looked right at home in such a get-up. He was in his middle fifties but was still pretty slender and about six feet tall. And I guess you could say he was distinguished looking despite the fact that his lips were so thin that they looked like two slices of ham. His eyes were mean, too, so cold they wouldn't have been out of place on a snake.

However, those defects were offset by a full head of iron gray hair and a matching mustache that he tended like it was a hanging garden of some sort. What's more, if you were a pretty girl, his eyes didn't look cold. They glowed like a tom-cat's. His whole face would glow, in fact. But if you were an old hard-tail boy like me, he would look at you in such a pained way you would think he had an infected adenoid.

When he got out of that station wagon, he was really pained. "No sign of him," he called out to Miss Maude and Cuba. "Hope for the worst. Maybe the undertow got him."

That's when I decided to brazen it out. I stepped out into the driveway and called out real cheerfully, "Looking for somebody?"

They all turned and stared at me. Then they got a good look at the suit and turned and stared at one another. Miss Maude took her glasses off and started cleaning them but the rest just stood there trying to think of something to say.

When I started up the steps, Cuba and Miss Maude bit their lips trying not to laugh. Laura just glared at me but Hamilton drew himself up and sneered, "Maude, just thank God that he didn't catch you on the beach. He seems to have stripped every other woman he met."

"John, shame on you!" Miss Maude said. Then she smiled at me. "Peter, dear, where did you get that *divine* suit?"

For her sake I didn't knock her brother out in the flower bed. "You really like it?" I said, holding out the skirt. "Some boys on a fishing boat gave it to me. They've got a sister who's either got gland trouble or has run off and joined a circus."

Cuba started laughing and Hamilton snarled for her to stop it. She kept laughing and went in the house. He glared at me again and followed her.

Then Laura snapped, "I want to talk to you, Farrell. *Privately!* Excuse us, Miss Maude."

She swished through the front door into the big center hall and saw Hamilton and Cuba in the Red Parlor on the left. He was raising hell with her and she was still laughing in his face. Laura must have realized they would interfere with her lecture so she started up the stairs.

"Follow me, Farrell!"

It was a pleasure. She had a movement that would make a Swiss watchmaker weep with envy and, going up the steps admiring it, I couldn't help thinking what a tragedy it was that Ben Ponza had lied to me about her.

She was 24, maybe, and the type of bouncy, sunshine blonde that you see in the outdoor ads driving speedboats and convertibles. Her eyes were a deep blue and twinkled or glinted, depending on your behavior. She wore her hair, which was naturally wavy, in a fluffy, tousled bob and her over-all effect was that of a real nice, pretty girl who could be an awful lot of fun, especially if you could ever persuade her to be a real bad girl.

As for her figure, it didn't catch your eye as fast as Cuba's, but once it did, and you gave it a little study, you realized that it was a masterpiece of its kind: a sports car chassis with Rolls Royce accessories.

At the top of the stairs she turned to the right. The big stairwell had rooms opening onto it like a court. With the only daylight being furnished by a couple of alcove windows, it was about as cheery as a furnished tomb, even at high noon.

Laura's room was the left corner one of the four across the front and she ushered me into it like it was criminal court. It was on the same order as just about every other room in the house: eighteen-foot ceilings, enough floor space to store government wheat, and old antique furniture so big that any piece of it would wear out a dust rag.

The outstanding attractions, though, were *two* big four-poster canopied beds. Miss Maude had told us some wild tale about her grandmother ordering the second one when grandfather came back from the war with a wooden leg and a weak kidney. The kidney got him up so much at night that he started wearing the leg to bed.

Laura prissed across the room, took her stand in front of the French doors opening onto the porch and started snapping at me again. "Pete Farrell, do you know what that Cuba said to me when she came back from the beach without her suit? And said it right in front of John Hamilton and Miss Maude?"

I cringed. "What?"

"She leered at me and said, 'Laura, sugar, you've spoiled him. I tried to tell him that *all* girls didn't take off their suits when they went to the beach but he wouldn't believe me.'"

She pointed to the door.

"Now, you just march yourself right back downstairs and tell them that I never saw you before in my life until yesterday and that I've certainly never been to any beach with you. What are you anyway? A sex maniac?"

"No," I said, "I'm just the damn fool who believed Ben Ponza when he wrote me that *you* were a sex maniac."

"Me?" she gasped. "Ben Ponza wrote you that I was a ...?"

I told her to hold it just a second. I cut through the bathroom, went into my room and came back with Ben's letter. I had been carrying it around for morale purposes. "I'll read it to you," I said, "and then you can apologize for using that door of yours last night for a guillotine."

She snatched the letter away and started reading it herself. When she came to the line where Ben said how much I would enjoy her favors, she started blushing. When she came to the line where he said that the only thing she didn't know about making love was when to stop, she tore the letter up and threw it in the wastebasket by the dressing table. She said that she could kill Ben.

"I really could. He *told* me he was going to write you that but I never dreamed he really would." Then she couldn't help laughing. "Ben's awful. And I don't blame you about Cuba. She's awful, too. As for that door act of yours last ..."

"Let's get back to Ben," I said. "He didn't also tell you something about Hamilton and a girl named Mary Belle Clayton, did he?"

It was a good thing I was watching her so closely. There was just a flicker of panic in her eyes and then she was herself again. "Mary *who?*" she said.

"Mary Belle Clayton."

"Oh, *her*. She was John Hamilton's secretary. The last one. The one before Cuba."

"What happened to her?"

"She died about two months ago."

I began to get that old feeling. Bloody Ben had struck again.

"How did she die?"

"In a hurricane."

"How in a hurricane?" I snapped. "For somebody who was raising so much hell a minute ago, you sure clammed up all of a sudden."

She laughed apologetically as though she didn't know she had clammed up. "But all I know is what Ben told me. He just said that she was going from here over to Queensport and her boat swamped and she drowned."

"A girl by herself in a boat in a *hurricane?*"

"Maybe it wasn't *in* the hurricane. I think Ben said it was the day before the hurricane hit but the bay was rough." She stared at me. "Why? What are you driving at? You sound like there's some mystery to it."

I told her to sit down. She kept acting puzzled and sat down on the end of the old green chaise longue. I gave her a sketchy account of what had happened on the beach with Cuba. She thought it was a lot funnier than I did. Then I gave her a detailed account of my little get-together with Harney Stokes and his brothers. I told her how they hated Hamilton, how they wouldn't tell me why they and everybody else around did hate him but that Puss had given me a hint just before they pulled out. "He told me to ask Hamilton what had *really* happened to Mary Belle."

She thought that was funny, too. "Is that all?" she laughed. "And you think there's some mystery to it? Boy, I'll bet you hated it when they took Crime Photographer off the air."

I told her to stop stalling. "If there isn't something fishy about this thing, why did Ben Ponza want me to come down here so bad that he was willing to lie to me about you being a sex maniac?"

"Oh, that's simple," she smiled. She got up and walked over to the dressing table and started messing with her hair. "You being so big and beautiful, he just assumed that I would turn into one. Like Cuba has."

"No," I said. "You mean that with me being so stupid and gullible and such a patsy for a pretty girl, he figured I would forget that he'd never sent me on any assignment that I didn't come back from with scabs." I told her about some of the other jobs that he had given me and then I walked over to her, took her by the shoulders and turned her around.

"And this is another one of those jobs. He knows something about this Mary Belle business and he's afraid you might get messed up in it and get your pretty head bashed in. He sent me along to see that you didn't."

She shook my hands loose from her shoulders. "Honestly," she said, "just how hard did that wave dump you on your head? Why in the world would John Hamilton want to drown somebody?"

"For the same reason that five of my fraternity brothers wanted to drown somebody once. Then the girl admitted that a sailor was the baby's daddy."

"Can't you think about anything but sex?" she sighed. "Besides, with John Hamilton's money don't you think he could take care of it?"

"Abortion? With John Hamilton's money maybe Mary Belle was more interested in the altar than alterations."

"Oh, stop it. You don't know a thing about the girl."

"But I'm going to find out."

She really got hot then. "Peter Farrell, you aren't going to do any such thing! If I do a good job on this story, Ben is going to send me to Paris for …"

"And send me to Lourdes, I guess. Heal the holes in my head. And you got a hole in yours. If you can pin a murder on the famous John Hamilton, the working girl's Faulkner, the last of the red-hot-southern gentlemen, Ben Ponza ought to buy Paris up and send it to you."

"Now, why would he want to pin anything on John Hamilton when they happen to be very dear friends? Ben was a guest here this summer and lots of times before that. And why would he send *me* down here on a murder story? Why not somebody from *Probe* or even one of his detective magazines?"

"Let's not be coy," I said. "Why did the Philistines send Delilah instead of a barber?" As for Ben having been a guest, I told her that that strengthened *my* case not hers. Ben would have seen Mary Belle and known what the setup was. And knowing the island and Hamilton and Jago, first hand, would be all the more justification for him to send me down to furnish fighter cover.

"And, furthermore," I said, "Hamilton isn't Ben Ponza's type. Hamilton is a phony and the one kind thing I can say about Ben Ponza at this moment is that he hates phonies. He wants you to pin something on Hamilton. Now, what is it? Why doesn't he want you to tell me?"

"Pete," she sighed, "why don't you go and get out of that idiotic bathing suit? Really, it's making an idiot out of you, too. You meet three strange fishermen, one of them merely tells you to ask John Hamilton—who's practically a stranger, too—what happened to his secretary, and, right away you start screaming bloody murder. You don't know the girl, you don't know any of the details, you don't know of any motive, you …"

"But I know Ben Ponza," I said. "I know he's never sent me on anything but a blood-letting yet. And I know he's going to pay for this. The other times I went knowingly. This time I go thinking that all I've got to do is take a few pictures and spend the rest of my time having fun with a pretty girl. But what happens? I …"

"You've *got* your pretty girl!" she snapped. "You've got Cuba."

She was looking in the dressing table mirror primping again. I put my hands lightly on her shoulders. "But I don't want Cuba," I said. "She's a maniac. I want you and I'm going to get you, Laura, dear."

She whirled away from me and started backing towards the door. "Pete, if you lay one finger on me …"

I couldn't help laughing. I told her that she knew damn well I'd never touch her unless she wanted me to. She knew it was the truth, too, but she still didn't like the way I was smiling. "Then just how do you propose going about *getting* me, Mr. Farrell?"

"It's real simple," I said. "Ben must think that this trouble is going to come to a head while we're down here. When it does, it's going to be a helluva lot worse than you think, and you're going to come knocking on *my* door. You're going to be scared, you're going to be begging my pardon and asking my protection.

"Ordinarily, I would be only too happy to protect you free of charge but because you've been so snippy and so stingy with your little secrets. I'll have to ask you to pay the supreme price."

She started smiling too … a taunting smile. "All right," she drawled. "We'll just make a little deal. *If* there is any trouble, if I ever come knocking at your door scared and asking your protection, I'll pay the supreme price.

"*But* until such time you won't badger John Hamilton about Mary Belle and you and I are just old pals. No hanky-panky. You're the photographer, I'm the writer and that's every bit of it. Strictly business. Okay?"

I stuck out my hand. "Shake, old pal."

She grinned and shook. I grinned, too. She seemed awfully sure of herself but from just the little I had already found out, I knew that monster Ben Ponza wouldn't let me down. There *was* going to be trouble and she *would* come knocking at my door!

CHAPTER THREE

After Laura and I made our bargain, I took a short-cut through the bathroom to my room. It was smaller than hers, but on the same order, except there was only one big canopied bed and its—the room's—most illustrious occupants had been Cuba, for a week, when she first moved in, and, a long time before that, great-uncle Danby Hamilton. According to Miss Maude, Uncle Danby had done most of the drinking for the family. Then, one fine summer evening he had taken on a load, tried to walk the railing to the second-story porch outside his room and his cargo had shifted. After sixty years of scrubbing, they still hadn't been able to get all of him off the brick walk where he landed.

I cleaned up, got dressed and went down to lunch. They were all waiting for me in the Green Parlor off the dining room and everybody but Hamilton had a smile for me. He had a snarl. "Mr. Farrell, I would like a word with you, if I may. *Alone.*" I told him, sure, and he headed for the library off the far end of the parlor. I winked at Miss Maude and followed him.

The library, being "his" room, was naturally the only comfortable one in the house. It was panelled in cherry and the chairs and things weren't any of these old antiques that looked like they had been designed for a man with a fused spine.

The panelling, where it wasn't taken up with book shelves, was hung with old maps, charts, hunting and fishing prints and pictures of him with some of his famous friends. On the wall over his desk was the thing that he seemed proudest of, and I guess it figured. It was a big old seaman's knife that he *claimed* had belonged to Blackbeard, a celebrated pirate of those parts at one time.

He took his stand in front of the stone fireplace that was big enough for Shadrach and Meshach to do an encore in, and arrogantly motioned me to a chair. He would feel more in command, glaring down at me instead of up at me. I accommodated him. I was going to be real polite and make friends with him so he would be easier to investigate.

"Mr. Farrell," he snapped, "I am well aware that photographers have a sexual boiling point even lower than that of sparrows and rabbits but I am still curious. Just what was this vile thing you did to my secretary this morning?"

There went my politeness. I boiled to my feet and told him that I hadn't done a damn thing to her that he hadn't done. "Only I probably did it a whole lot better!" I said. "Even when I was bouncing along on my head!"

That ended the discussion right there. It not only infuriated him, it baffled him, too. He glared at me, tried to think of something to say and then headed for the door.

"And one more thing!" I said. "You try playing secretary with Laura Ames and I'll leave your face looking so much like a pizza they'll put anchovies on it instead of bandages. And that goes for your trained ape, Jago, too."

He went through the door and put on a performance that made me wonder whether the Hamilton were descended from monkeys or chameleons. One second he was so mad he looked like he was going to be sick, the next second he was smiling and telling the ladies that the beach incident was closed and we just wouldn't refer to it again.

Lunch followed the same pattern that all our other meals had. Laura asked him about the new novel he had coming out, *Weep, the Phoenix,* and right away he turned lunch into a do-it-yourself testimonial dinner. He said he was quite pleased with *Phoenix.* A book club had it, one of Ben Ponza's magazines was serializing it for fifty thousand dollars and Hollywood had bought it for four hundred thousand.

There went my appetite. He had parlayed sex, symbolism and the Old South—the formula he always used—into another fortune. But that wasn't bad enough. He had to tell us the plot. The gist of it, as far as I could gather, was this:

A crippled, widowed plantation owner marries a young Scarlett O'Hara type. She winds up seducing all his sons, swipes his crutches and sets the house on fire. Then, she finds her latest lover's bones in the ashes, too. He had sneaked into the house to knock the old man off himself.

Finally, Hamilton had to stop to breathe and Miss Maude broke in and said that he'd better have Jago go down to the dock and check the boat. She'd heard over the radio that the northeaster was moving in and the storm warnings were going up.

I tried getting the talk around to hurricanes, in hopes that Mary Belle's name might be mentioned, but Miss Maude pooh-poohed the idea that a northeaster was in the same class. "Oh, the wind may build up to gusts of seventy miles an hour when we get the full brunt of it in the next day or so, but it won't compare to a hurricane, dear, believe me. Why the last one ..."

That's when Hamilton cut her off. He asked Laura if she wouldn't like to go riding after lunch and see the rest of the island while the weather was still decent. Laura cut her glance at me as though to say it was part of the job and told him that she thought it would be fun.

"But, John," Miss Maude said, "maybe Peter would like to go riding, too?"

He looked nauseated again and said, "These are saddle horses, dear." The implication was that, not being a gentleman, I'd never ridden anything but plowhorses or mules. "Besides," he added, "I'm sure that Mr. Farrell has work to do."

"Oh, he has," Cuba leered. "He didn't finish what he started this morning." She paused just long enough. "His picture taking, I mean."

About an hour later, she showed me what she really meant. Laura and Hamilton had gone for their ride, Miss Maude was taking a nap and I had my color camera set up in the Red Parlor. Then, just as I was getting ready to make a shot of the fancy marble fireplace, she came in with a big tray full of trouble: a bottle of bourbon, a bottle of vodka, and all the accessories.

She casually put it down on the table in front of the settee, went back, pulled the big sliding doors shut and then smiled and said: "Sugar, I hope you didn't mind my going into your room and getting some of your private stock. John went off with the key to ours but I knew you had some."

The reason she knew I had some was when I was unloading my luggage, on arriving, my biggest suitcase popped open and exposed all the weapons I had brought along to lay siege to Laura: bourbon, Scotch, gin, vodka, champagne, silk pajamas, the red nightgown, a book of love poems, an album called Boudoir Ballads, a honeymoon kit and a big bottle of pep pills. Laura had wanted to kill me.

And now I wanted to kill Cuba. As far as I was concerned that beach incident had made her the Typhoid Mary of the sex world. But I wanted her to be in a friendly mood when I asked her about Mary Belle, so instead of bouncing her out and locking the doors, I told her she was a real sweet girl.

She handed me the bottle of bourbon to open and said that I was sweet, too, especially for not being mad about the beach.

"You shouldn't have teased Cuba about her suit, though. She doesn't like to be teased."

That was like a rattlesnake saying it didn't like to be bitten. But I just smiled, gave the cork a twist and passed the bottle back. She winked at me.

"But don't you worry, sugar," she said. "Cuba's going to make it up to you. Miss Maude is taking a nap. After you make your little picture, we'll take the tray and the goodies up to your room." Then she grinned. "Cuba's been wanting to have some fun on one of those big old beds ever since she got here."

I couldn't resist it. "Well, what's Hamilton got in his room?" I said. "A hammock?"

"Sugar," she leered, "you don't think that if John Hamilton was making love to Cuba he would be wasting his time panting after your little blonde friend, do you?"

I stared at her and my spine began icing up. "Now, just one damn minute," I said.

She smiled. "I met that snobbish bastard at a cocktail party in Baltimore six weeks ago when he gave a lecture there. He was all set to court me until he discovered I wasn't anything but a secretary. Then he just decided to buy me. He leered at me and said that he would give me five hundred dollars a week to be *his* secretary."

"Did you say five hundred dollars a *week*?"

"That's all it was and he wanted typing, too. Why, sugar, just the night before, a nice old man had offered me a twenty-five thousand dollar a year salary and all his credit cards just to lie around a penthouse of his. And next month this sweet thing I know is taking me on a round-the-world cruise with him. Of course, he's going to marry me, too, but he doesn't know that yet."

"Cuba," I wheezed, "let me get this straight and don't get mad at me. John Hamilton is paying you a salary like that and you haven't been more than a secretary to him even *once*?"

She grinned and went on with her bartending. She said she was wild but she wasn't for sale. If she was, she would have her own secretaries. "I just decided to teach this arrogant, cheap sonofabitch a lesson, so I've been here for five weeks and all he's gotten from me is bad spelling and insomnia."

While she was saying that, all I could think of was our little scene in the library before lunch. That egomaniac— maybe a homicidal maniac, too—hadn't even touched his five-hundred-dollar-a-week secretary, and there I was telling him about making love to her even bouncing along on my head.

"Listen to me, Cuba," I pleaded. "You're gonna get us shot. You're gonna put your hand on my knee one more time, he's gonna get a gun and there'll be more fingers and knee caps flying around than …"

She laughed. "Sugar, he's not going to shoot anybody. He's a gentleman and a gentleman doesn't do that. Just like a gentleman doesn't admit that he's offered a secretary five hundred dollars a week for anything but clean carbons."

She passed me my drink. "That's all I've been hanging around here for. I want to see just how long before he drops this gentleman routine and starts being the nasty old man he really is."

"Well, I've got news for you," I said. "It could be any minute now and you don't know just how nasty an old man he can be. Mary Belle Clayton didn't know either."

That ran her grin to half-mast. "Mary Belle Clayton? She's …"

I finished it for her. "She's dead." I glanced towards the doors to make certain they were shut and sat down beside her. I told her about my run-in with the Stokes brothers, my discussion with Laura and how the whole thing was adding up to just the type of job that Ben Ponza would send me on.

"Laura knows something about Mary Belle," I said, "but she won't tell me what. Now what do you know?"

For once she was serious. She said that all she knew was what Jago had told her and he made it sound so tragic that she hadn't mentioned it to Hamilton. He and Miss Maude had made some casual references to Mary Belle but they had never mentioned the drowning itself. She shook her head.

"Sugar, I'd like to tie that can to John Hamilton's tail but I'm afraid it's just one of those Queensport rumors. They hate him over there."

"But what was Mary Belle doing out in a boat by herself in a hurricane?"

She confirmed Laura's version. It had been the day before the hurricane hit and she was going home for the week-end like she always did.

"But there wasn't any reason she shouldn't have been out by herself," she added. "She was raised on Queen's Bay. Jago said she could handle a boat as good as any man."

"But what kind of boat was she in? Maybe the hurricane hadn't hit but the bay was still rough enough to swamp a boat. Why didn't Jago take her over in the cruiser?"

"He couldn't get it started and she didn't want to wait until he could fix whatever was wrong. She took the small boat they had. But it wasn't too small. Jago said she could have made it easy if she had stayed in the lee of those little islands between here and over there. Instead she cut right across the open water and …"

"Wait a minute," I said. "People who are raised around water have got more respect for it than anybody, but Mary Belle heads out across two miles of rough open water in a …"

"Sugar, maybe she was just stupid. Not *everybody* raised around water is a brain." She was getting bored with it and I couldn't blame her too much but I kept fishing.

"Well, if she was stupid why did Jago let her go."

"I *don't* know. All I know is that her boat must have swamped and that was the last anybody ever saw of her."

Now, I thought, that was right interesting. "The last *anybody* ever saw of her?" I said. "You mean the body never washed in?"

She sampled her drink and sighed. "Her body didn't wash in, but so what? Maybe it was carried out to sea. Maybe it washed up in a marsh fifty miles from here. This *was* a hurricane, you know."

"I know," I said, "and if I was on an island and had a nagging, pregnant young friend I wanted to dispose of, I can't think of anything that would come in handier than a nice hurricane. Knock her on the head, dump her out at sea and then tell everybody that the last I saw of her she was trying to beat the hurricane home. The perfect crime!"

"So forget it," Cuba said. "Even if there was some truth to it, all he has to say is, where's the body?"

"Maybe Ben knows something. Maybe it's been recovered. Maybe he didn't weight her down good enough and ...'

"Oh, stop," she said. "Why would he want to weight her down? He would *want* the body to wash in. It would prove she had drowned but it wouldn't prove that *he* had drowned her."

"But who said he drowned her? Maybe Mary Belle had finger marks on her throat. Maybe she had three eyes, one in the middle with a .38 slug for an eyeball."

"All right, Sherlock," she said, giving me a pained smile, "you've convinced me. *Except* for one little thing. I forgot to mention that Miss Maude was down at the dock with John Hamilton and Jago and saw Mary Belle off. Now, do you think she would cover up for any murder? And do you think she is going to nap all afternoon?"

As far as she was concerned that settled the case against John Hamilton. She got to her feet and got real cozy. "Let's go up, sugar. You can play with your little camera later. Play with Cuba now."

I looked up at her. She really did want to play and it suddenly occurred to me why. She had been leading such a virtuous, sexless life torturing Hamilton that she had become tortured herself. Now, ordinarily, nobody is more willing to help out a pretty, sexually underprivileged girl than I am, but she had forfeited my sympathy. She could have remedied her condition on the beach that morning but she just couldn't pass up the opportunity to be bitchy and torture me. We were both in the same boat now, but this time I had the oars. Besides that, I wasn't about to have Hamilton, as mad as he must still be, come back unexpectedly and walk in on us. Sheet burns I didn't mind, but powder burns were something else.

"Cuba," I said, "I don't think Miss Maude would cover up for a murder either. But maybe Hamilton had done something to the boat. Maybe …"

"Don't be mean!"

She said it with so much feeling that I knew I had diagnosed her condition. And she seemed to sense that, too, because she got real sweet again. "Please, don't tease Cuba. She's not going to tease you any more. We don't have to go upstairs. Cuba can lock those doors and …"

"Have you ever seen a picture of Mary Belle?" I asked. "She was real pretty, I bet."

She leaned down, took my face in her hands and kissed me. Inside me all these little voices started crying out. One said, "Oh, you fool, you! Lock those doors!" But a little louder one said: "You do and that maniac will ride up and shoot you through the window!"

Cuba finally unpuckered.

"Now?" she murmured.

"No," I croaked and before she could finish me off there was a knock on the door. It was Miss Maude. "Peter, may I come in, dear?"

"Just a second, Miss Maude," I gasped. "I'll open up."

"Hurry up and get rid of her," Cuba whispered.

I whispered back that I wasn't going to be impolite. "I'm going to give her a few drinks and find out what she knows about Mary Belle."

For a second I thought she was going to claw me but then she settled for a snarl.

"Damn, you! You just wait!"

She heard Miss Maude sliding the doors open herself and straightened up and started smiling and messing with her dress. "Am I glad to see you," she said. "He's really awful, Miss Maude. Don't let him close those doors on you."

Miss Maude tittered that she didn't believe a word of it. Then she spotted the tray. "Oh, you're having a tea party. Am I invited?" I told her she sure was and went out in the butler's pantry to get her a glass. When I got back she said that Cuba had gone into the library to do a little work.

"Good," I said. "Now, it'll come out even. A bottle for me and a bottle for you." I thought I was kidding but she took her glass and proceeded to pour herself a drink that looked like it was meant for an alcoholic camel.

"It's the only thing that helps my arthritis," she smiled, when she saw me staring at the size of it. "Just seems to loosen me right up."

I started to warn her that a drink that big would loosen up the Cardiff Giant, but since I wanted to get her tipsy enough to tell me about Mary Belle I didn't say anything. I just made a grab for my own glass but she beat me to it. She poured me the same size dose, ignored the soda and ginger ale and handed it over. "We don't have to put anything else in these, do we, dear?"

I hesitated and then said, "No, ma'am." The drink was going to make me the first man into space, I knew that, but I was more worried about what Hamilton would say when he got back. Defiling his secretary was one thing, passing out poor old Miss Maude was something else.

"Well, here goes," she said. "Geronimo!"

Two hours later I had shot pictures in the two parlors, the library—complete with Cuba—and was in the dining room. By talking about the storm moving in, I had got Miss Maude on the subject of their last hurricane and she had told me a lot of interesting things about Hamilton, Mary Belle and the day of the tragedy.

But I wasn't conscious of having played the detective so well. All I was conscious of was that the bourbon had been killed, the vodka mortally wounded and I was just about a litter case myself. I was sitting at the dining-room table about to fall on my face and "poor, old Miss Maude" was hopping around, laughing, hollering "watch the birdie," and taking pictures of me.

When she wasn't telling me to quit crossing my eyes, she was telling me about the book we were going to do together. It was going to be about the island and her ancestors and the various ghosts that had haunted the house. I think I had suggested the idea when we hit the library but I wasn't sure.

Finally, it occurred to me that I was sitting there taking orders—"Peter, get your chin up off your chest, dear"—from a photographer who was about to wreck a two-thousand-dollar color camera. That sobered me up enough to tell her that we'd better knock off work for the day. She said, fine, she would take me up to her room and show me what our book was going to be like.

She then put the last of the vodka into a couple of Lawdy Maudies, a vodka-and-blackberry-wine-concoction she had named after herself but should have named after General MacArthur. Every time you got one halfway down you could hear it saying, "I shall return."

So we polished those two off and the next thing I knew she was helping me up the steps. We were singing "Onward, Christian Soldiers" and making so much noise that Mattie, Jago's wife, had come to the bottom of the steps to see what was wrong.

Then, I was sitting in a big chair in Miss Maude's room. She was pulling out a lot of drawers looking for something, but before I could find out what it was, the bourbon and the vodka and the Lawdy Maudies started fighting among themselves.

I staggered to my feet and told Miss Maude I though I had better go to my room. She started to protest but then she saw that I looked like I had swallowed a yo-yo and said perhaps it would be best.

She may have helped me to my bed. I wasn't sure, but that's where I woke up about two hours later. Outside it was dark and I could hear the wind blowing. Then, next door in Miss Maude's room, I could hear voices. It sounded like an argument. I figured that Hamilton was back and raising hell with my little playmate and maybe I had better see about helping her out.

I got to my feet and didn't feel as bad as I should have, mainly because I was still half drunk. I crossed the room and eased my door open. One of the voices was Hamilton's all right. He was shouting about something but I still couldn't make out what he was saying. Then the door opened and he backed out into the hall. Miss Maude said something and then he really cut loose.

"All right!" he shouted. "All right! But find it, goddammit, find it!"

He turned and stared coming up the hall. I closed my door almost shut and watched him go past. His face looked like ten miles of bad road. But something puzzled me. He didn't look just mad, he looked panicky, too. I went into the bathroom and tapped on Laura's door.

"Just pals?" she called out.

I sighed and said, yes, and went in.

She had on a crisp, fresh blue dress and was standing in front of the dressing table mirror fixing her hair and looking like something every man dreams of sharing a bedroom with. She didn't turn around. Just looked at me in the mirror and snapped, "Pete Farrell, just *what* did you do to Miss Maude?"

I groaned and told her that was like asking Lincoln what he did to Booth. "*She* got me drunk," I said. "She's got a stomach lined with dust. Now, you tell me something. What was all that hell Hamilton was raising just now?"

She still didn't turn around. "You know that book you two were going to do about the island?"

I nodded. I remembered vaguely. I was going to do the pictures for it … *if* there was anything left of my camera.

"Well," Laura said, "it was going to be based on a journal, one of those diary type things, that Miss Maude has been keeping for about a year."

I didn't remember that part. "But what was Hamilton so mad about?"

"He had no idea she was keeping it. When we came back, he asked Mattie how things had gone. She said that you two had a real party and that Miss Maude had taken you up to her room to show you some book she had been writing on the sly. John went up and demanded to see it and she told him it was nothing but a journal and she couldn't find it. She had misplaced it. He got furious."

"But why?"

"Because he said that she was trying to capitalize on his name getting a book published. He said he was not going to have his private life exploited."

That didn't make sense. What were we doing but exploiting his private life for *Chic* magazine? He loved stories about his little kingdom by the sea. And, if you had enough circulation, there wasn't much he wouldn't tell you. I walked over to Laura.

"And this is a journal, a diary sort of, she's been keeping?"

She nodded. "Sort of. But she was writing it with a book in mind. It's about life on the island, the birds, the seasons, the guests they have down. But John thinks it's mostly about him."

"Turn around and look at me," I said.

She acted annoyed but she turned around. I took a good look into her eyes.

"Thanks," I said. "That's all I want to know."

I walked back into my room. She hadn't been able to hide it. She knew something was wrong, too. And I thought I knew what it was. John Hamilton was acting mad and scared, both, about that journal for just one reason: He was afraid that Miss Maude might innocently have put something in it that would throw some light on what really had happened to Mary Belle Clayton.

CHAPTER FOUR

By the time I got showered, shaved and dressed, the wind had started whistling, and outside, in the lights from the house, I could see the oaks swaying to the tune. Somewhere a limb was scraping the tin roof and a shutter was banging. It was such a fine hour for contemplating dark deeds that I got my harp—mouth organ, to some people—out of my suitcase and sat down in a chair by the window and started playing and trying to recall all the things that Miss Maude had told me before I had been taken suddenly drunk. Right in the middle of "The Coffin in the Baggage Car Up Ahead," a piece I do particularly well, Laura knocked on the door.

I hollered for her to come in. Ordinarily, I would have been a gentleman and ushered her in but I could tell from the knock that she was going to give me trouble. And she did. She said my harp playing sounded like a cat in pain. Then she said they were waiting on me downstairs. "What are you doing? You aren't *still* drunk?"

I sighed and got to my feet and told her that I was improving. I was now only three-eighths drunk. As to what I had been doing, I had been staying out of Cuba's clutches and putting some more pieces in my puzzle.

"Miss Maude confirmed my suspicions," I said. "Mary Belle Clayton was twenty-two years old, blonde, good looking and stupid. She was in love with John Hamilton and thought he was in love with her. Miss Maude says she tried to warn her but she …"

Laura took me by the arm and started leading me towards the door. "When children start killing Santa Claus, then John Hamilton will start killing good-looking, twenty-two-year-old blondes. Now, come on and leave that dreary harp here or he really will ask you to leave."

I put the harp in my pocket and told her that he couldn't ask me to leave. I was now Miss Maude's guest, not his.

"That's something else I found out," I said. "Miss Maude's father left her half the island and half the house and left Hamilton the same thing. *But* to protect Miss Maude from her loving brother, he left her the half of the island that has the house on it."

She couldn't help but smile at that. "You made that up."

"Ask Hamilton," I said. "If he gives Miss Maude any trouble, she can ban him from her half of the island, which would mean that he couldn't get to his half of the house. So there's another piece in the puzzle. Even Hamilton's own father didn't trust him."

"All right," she sighed, "maybe he is an ass but he's not any murderer or whatever you think he is. So, don't antagonize him. *Please?*"

I told her I wouldn't unless he antagonized me. And as soon as we got downstairs that was just what he proceeded to do. He popped to his feet and asked me if I had seen his sister's so-called journal. He wasn't being especially impolite to me, but he was to Miss Maude and that made it worse. She was sitting there smiling and being real gracious and still belting away at the whiskey. Anybody who could ramble like she could deserved everybody's respect.

So I asked Hamilton what he meant by *so-called* journal.

"I'll bet it's a classic."

"Mr. Farrell," he said, "I am not in the habit of asking photographers for literary opinions. I asked if you happen to see the journal."

Miss Maude told him to stop. "Dear, I merely misplaced it. It's still in that big old messy room of mine some place. I just can't understand you being so exercised about this."

He ignored that and asked me again if I had seen it when I was in the room. He was almost making it sound like I had taken it.

"Look," I said, "I was so full of Lawdy Maudies I couldn't have seen a set of encyclopedias, much less a journal." Then, I told him I couldn't understand why he objected so to Miss Maude's writing about life on the island, her ancestors, and all. "You got a copyright on the subject?"

Miss Maude laughed and said that she had asked him the same thing. He had written such horrible things in his books about the island and members of the family that she was certainly entitled to write some nice things. Then, she addressed herself to Laura:

"Did you read that perfectly terrible thing of his, *The Fickle Shore*? He disguised it somewhat, of course, but that was about great-aunt Polly. She was a perfect lady except for one little fling with a sea captain but John made her into one of those creatures that ..."

"A nymphomaniac," Cuba said. She had been sitting there glaring at me and not saying anything, but she couldn't resist a passing bite at Hamilton.

"Thank you, dear," Miss Maude said. "He made her one of those and every time she got the urge she would dash down to the beach and start yoo-hooing at any sailor that happened to be passing. When he wrote that, I just decided that I would write a *nice* book about life on the island and bring out little anecdotes to prove that the Hamiltons were very fine people and not the dreadful creatures John has made them out. So I started keeping my little journal."

I thought it was right sad and so did Laura but Hamilton didn't. He acted as though it was ridiculous. "I have written seventeen novels," he said to Laura. "In any of them, have you ever seen the name Hamilton mentioned? Or this island? Of course you haven't but Maude insists ..." He laughed as though she was getting senile. "... she insists on seeing the Hamiltons in everything I write."

"Dear," Miss Maude smiled patiently, "you haven't used names, of course, but I know who you mean. And so do *they*."

"Oh, for God's sake!" Hamilton snorted. He turned to Laura again. "Do you know who she means by *they*? You remember the family cemetery we passed? On the banks of the little creek? Well, that's who she means by *they*. The occupants. She insists I won't let them rest in peace. I am blessed, or maybe it's cursed, with the powers of resurrection. My novels, *supposedly* about them, have brought them back from the dead to haunt us."

He started laughing. "Now, do you wonder why I insist on seeing what she has written?" He turned to Miss Maude and explained that that was the only reason he had gotten so upset. "You find your little classic and let me look it over and if I don't think you've made us all too ridiculous with your ghosts, I'll even *help* you get it published."

He had changed his tune. At first, he hadn't wanted his private life exploited. Now, he didn't want Miss Maude's stupidity exposed. It sounded better that way but I still had the feeling that he was damn anxious to see whatever it was she had written. I glanced at Laura to see what her reaction was, but good old Cuba broke things wide open.

"Miss Maude," she said, sweetly, "I don't think your ghosts are ridiculous at all. Tell Laura about the one who looks like Mary Belle. Maybe she'll see her tonight."

Hamilton couldn't take any more. "Cuba, goddammit, stop it! Why must you encourage her?"

Well, that took care of the journal and the ghosts for a while but not the friction. I sat down with Miss Maude and Cuba to find out some more about the ghost that looked like Mary Belle but then I overheard Hamilton say something to Laura about senile old women and drunken photographers. I rose to the challenge. I took a big drink and whipped out my harp. I gave a warm-up blast on the shrill end and he nearly jumped out of his chair.

"Great God! What was *that?*"

I ignored him and played such cheery little numbers as "The Rosewood Casket," "The Letter Edged in Black" and "Her Mother Turned Her Picture to the Wall." Miss Maude and Cuba cheered me to the rafters and begged for more—partly because they appreciated fine music and partly because they could see what it was doing to Hamilton. He was ready to climb the drapes.

When I did "Listen To the Mockingbird" with Miss Maude coming in on the breaks as the mockingbird—she could whistle almost as well as I could play—he hollered out and asked Mattie what the hell was keeping dinner.

Dinner wasn't any better. Thanks to Miss Maude, I was about five-eighths drunk again and, when Hamilton launched into some story about himself and Hemingway, I turned to Miss Maude and asked if she thought Mary Belle's ghost was going to walk that night.

"Maybe I can get a picture of her," I said. And, as I said it, I heard Hamilton pause as though he was going to bellow again but he decided he would just ignore it.

"Well, dear," Miss Maude said, very seriously, "it would be so nice if you could get a picture of her but I'm not sure you could. At times you seem to sense her rather than see her. Don't you think so, Cuba? Cuba's seen her too, you know. On a night just like this one, wasn't it, child? Oh, this is a grand night for them, just grand. Tell him, Cuba."

Cuba seemed as serious as Miss Maude but I didn't believe a word she said. The wind was beginning to howl outside, we were eating by candlelight and there were these spooky, shadows dancing on the wall. I think she was just trying to scare Laura.

"Well, he might be able to get a picture of her," she said. "You remember I moved out of the room that Pete's in now because I saw her in there. I saw her then, just as plainly as I see Laura." That was to get Laura's attention. "But the second time, about three weeks ago, when we had that real windy night, I did just seem to sense that she was there. But there wasn't any doubt about it She *was* in the room."

I could hear Hamilton's voice taking on more of an edge. And, out of the corner of my eye, I could see that Laura was taking more of an interest in our talk about ghosts than she was in Hamilton's about Hemingway.

"But, Miss Maude," I said, "are you sure it's Mary Belle?"

"Well, I'm not *positive*. You know I don't see well at all without my glasses, especially in the dark, and she always seems to vanish so quickly. I even tried sleeping with my glasses on, one night, but …"

That did it. Hamilton banged his hand down on the table. "By God, Maude, I will not have a guest subjected to this!"

"But I think she finds it quite interesting, don't you, dear?" Laura gave her a weak little smile that could have meant anything. "Certainly you do," Miss Maude went on. "I was telling Peter that I'm not *positive* that this particular ghost is Mary Belle, but since she does have her coloring and didn't appear until after the tragedy I just assume that …"

Cuba interrupted her. "Miss Maude, listen. Shhhh …"

She was leaning back slightly in her chair and looking into the parlor as though she was trying to see the ceiling. The urgent tone of her voice and the strange way she was acting made everybody uneasy.

"You hear one?" I wheezed.

"Goddammit, Farrell, stop it!" Hamilton snapped. "Cuba, why must you do this?" He turned to Laura in disgust. "This never happens until the whiskey starts flowing, and if it's not a case of nocturnal d.t.'s, I …"

"Oh, stop spluttering!" Cuba said. "There's someone in my room."

Her room was partly over the parlor but the way the old floors creaked you could hear somebody overhead two or three rooms away. And there *was* somebody in her room—somebody trying to ease around and not doing too quiet a job of it. Hamilton tried to ignore it. "Nonsense! It's the wind. Now, will you …?"

"Wind?" I said. "With feet that big?"

He sighed and listened, too. Suddenly, he was being real sporting. He smiled at Cuba. "My apologies." Then he reached over and patted Laura's hand. "It's Jago. I told him to check the windows and the shutters."

Laura laughed and told him she was disappointed. Which was a lie. She hadn't been breathing the whole time. Then, she told him she'd always wanted to see a real, genuine, old, southern-mansion type ghost. Hamilton smiled and told her just to keep listening to Miss Maude. "She'll have you seeing them whether they are there or not, won't you, dear?"

Miss Maude started to say something but all of a sudden he was on a charm jag. He started talking to everybody instead of just Laura, telling these tales about how Miss Maude had frightened various guests clean off the island. It was right funny and I, even, laughed but then I noticed Cuba. She was still listening to the creaking going on in her room but she was having a hard time hearing anything. That started me wondering. Was Hamilton making all that noise because he didn't *want* her to hear anything?

I leaned over and asked Miss Maude if she didn't want me to "sweeten" the drink she had brought to the table. She smiled and nodded and I took the glass, excused myself and went back into the parlor where the whiskey was. Hamilton was going full blast so I didn't have to worry about him. I eased out of the parlor into the hall and very quietly made my way up the stairs.

The upstairs was gloomy enough in the day time and at night, with no light except that from a few little snake-neck lamps along the walls, it was so eerie that a ghost would have to have guts to haunt it. But this time there was a little more light—the light in Cuba's room was on and the door was about half open.

From the top of the stairs I could see into it at an angle; part of the big bed, a chair, the night table and a chest of drawers. Then Jago eased into view. What a comforting sight he was! Six feet seven, two hundred and sixty pounds or so and all dumb brute: dark, swarthy; little bloodshot gray eyes; broad nose; a low, split-level forehead and a mat of short black hair that fit his head the way moss fits a rock.

Night-time did the same sort of thing for him that it did for the upstairs. He looked bigger, uglier and meaner than ever. At first, I thought he was through checking the windows and was coming out. But, then, he paused by the bed as though he was listening for something. Then he turned his attention to the big chair. He lifted the seat cushion, looked under it and put it back in place. Then he got down on his knees and started looking under the bed. That was all I wanted to know. I headed down the stairs.

Back in the parlor, I fixed Miss Maude a drink that couldn't help but put her to bed earlier. Then I casually strolled back into the dining room. Hamilton was still being the charmer, still tell-ing stories about various guests they'd had down. He didn't even glance at me when I sat back down so I figured that he hadn't been doing any fretting about my absence.

Miss Maude, though, welcomed me back, sampled the drink, pronounced it very tasty, and got back in the party.

"But, Laura," she said, breaking in on Hamilton, "the most dreadful thing we ever had happen was with your friend, Mr. Ponza. Don't you dare breathe a word of it, though. It was simply ghastly. I don't see why he didn't kill John, really."

It was the first time I had ever heard Hamilton really cut loose and laugh so I knew he must have done something real jolly to our Ben. I was awfully glad I had come back when I did.

"You mean on Ben's trip down here this summer?" Laura asked Miss Maude.

"Oh, no, child. This was in the fall about five years ago. John had this big deer hunt for his friends. They came from all over and John told them to be sure and bring their wives or their lady friends down. Jago and I would take them cruising on John's new boat while the men hunted.

"Well, poor Ben made the mistake of bringing his fiancée down: not knowing, mind you, that among the other couples John had invited, were *two* of Ben's ex-wives."

Laura's mouth fell open and she stared at Hamilton as though she was realizing, for the first time, just how right I had been about him. But she recovered and managed a laugh.

"Oh, you're awful! I don't see why he *didn't* kill you!"

Hamilton managed to stop laughing long enough to say that he had really done Ben a favor. "The girl just wasn't his type. Completely unsophisticated. No background."

"Well, he certainly wasn't *her* type after those two ex-wives of his got through telling her about him," Miss Maude said. "I never felt so sorry for a man in my life. It cost him the girl and she was lovely, really. How John kept his friendship after that I'll never know."

"It's quite simple, dear," Hamilton said. "Just ask him some time what a Hamilton serial can do for the circulation of his magazines."

That ended the Hour of Charm. After dinner we adjourned to the parlor where things went just the way I hoped they wouldn't. Hamilton maneuvered Laura into the library again, telling her that he was afraid I was going to start playing my harp again and his digestion was delicate enough as it was. Then, Miss Maude broke out the cards and suggested that she and Cuba and I take up that miserable rummy game of hers where we had left off the night before.

Cuba took her literally. She had been sore at me when I had first come down, and for about a half hour after hearing Jago in her room she had been real quiet and preoccupied, but as soon as we sat down at that card table she started smiling and torturing me the way she had during our first game.

She would slip a shoe off under the table and stick a warm, silky foot up my pants leg and wiggle her toes. Then, when she would "knock" out in the game, she would lean over to see what cards I had and would always get one of my hands pinned under her breasts. It was like having it in a pressure cooker, and every time she touched me I'd glance towards the library door to see if old five-hundred-a-week Hamilton was watching.

Finally, around 10:30, Miss Maude started dropping her cards on the floor and knocking drinks over. Then, she said she thought she would have a little nightcap—she'd had three already—and go on up. So she tossed it off and I escorted her up to her room and something prompted me to give her a little good-night kiss on the forehead. Maybe it was my conscience.

She was such a nice old lady that I was beginning to feel ashamed of myself for the sadness I might be bringing her.

"That was sweet, dear," she said smiling up at me. "Now, I'm going to find that journal and we'll start making plans for our book the first thing tomorrow."

I told her, fine, closed the door and went back downstairs. As soon as I hit the parlor, I wanted to weep. Cuba had turned out all the lights and the glow from the fireplace had turned everything soft and cozy. She was sitting on the rug in front of the fire looking like some sort of Aphrodite of the Flames.

She smiled up at me and patted the rug. "Sit down by Cuba, sugar."

If we had been any place but Hamilton's house I would have made one pounce and that fine old oriental rug would have wound up looking like a bath mat. Instead, I turned on the floor lamp by the couch behind her and then tiptoed over to the library door and listened. Hamilton was telling Laura about a deer hunt he was going to take her on in the morning. I eased back over to the fireplace and sat down by Cuba. Not right beside her but out of her reach on a hassock.

"Sugar," she pouted, leaning towards me, "you promised, that after you talked to Miss Maude this afternoon, you would play with Cuba. Now, why do you keep fighting it?"

"For three damn good reasons," I said, lowering my voice. "For one thing, you're not using me as a red flag to wave in that bull's face any more. He's right in that next room and he's got a big knife on the wall over his desk and I want it to stay on the wall.

"For another thing, he doesn't think Miss Maude misplaced that journal. He thinks one of us has got it and he's had Jago going through our rooms hunting for it. Now, if there wasn't something to this Mary Belle business, and if he wasn't afraid that Miss Maude might have innocently put something in that journal that might arouse somebody's suspicions, why would he have Jago hunting for it? And why would he be so upset about it?"

She went into her long-suffering act again. "Pete, Jago was checking my windows and making sure the shutters wouldn't bang."

I got off the hassock and sat down beside her. "Well, you got damn strange windows," I said. "Under your bed and in the seat of your chair. That's where he was checking when I saw him."

I explained how I had sneaked upstairs during dinner and seen him in her room. "And you *knew* he was doing something in your room besides checking windows. I watched you."

"Oh, that," she said, not pretending that she wasn't puzzled by the other. "I missed some money about two weeks ago. I thought I might be about to miss some more. And how do you know Jago wasn't just hunting for my handbag? I've started hiding it now."

"Under your bed? Hanging from the slats?"

She smiled a little at that and then shook her head. "Even if he was hunting for the journal, you're silly thinking it's got anything to do with Mary Belle. You know how Miss Maude can say these wild things that embarrass John. He's probably just afraid that she may have written something about him that his friends would die laughing at if they ever got their hands on the journal. If he really had Jago searching our rooms, that's the reason."

"Maybe," I said, "but you didn't see his face this afternoon after he got through bellowing at Miss Maude. He wasn't just mad, he was scared. And it wasn't just because he was thinking that some of his friends might get to read something funny about him."

"But what could she write about him and Mary Belle that would scare him? After all, she was going to show it to you and you know she wouldn't show anybody anything that would hurt her precious brother."

"Not intentionally, no. But maybe she made a slip. Maybe the day she was supposed to have seen Mary Belle off at the dock, she was sick in bed or something. And maybe she put down in the journal that she was sick in bed all day. The police would find that real interesting, I think.

"Or maybe she jotted down something that Hamilton did during the hurricane. It might just seem funny to her but to the police it might seem that he was getting ready to dispose of a body or ..."

I stopped. Cuba wasn't listening any more. She was just sitting there looking smug. "Then you did ask her about seeing Mary Belle off at the dock? And she said she did see her off, didn't she?"

I sighed and admitted it. "She said she was there but she was damn hazy about it. And you know damn good and well that the way she drinks there might be days when she's so hazy she doesn't know where she is. She could have drawn a blank that day and then just taken Hamilton's word for it that she was at the dock—rather than admit to him that she didn't remember. She knows how he feels about her drinking too much."

She ignored that and looked up at me real dreamy and asked me if I wouldn't please stop it. "Pete, *please*," she murmured. "You know you want to finish what we started this morning."

"Cuba, listen to me," I said. "I told you I had *three* reasons why I wasn't going to take a chance around John Hamilton. I've told you two of 'em. Now, my third and biggest reason, the one that makes me certain that ..."

I didn't get to finish. I had been so intent on telling her my third reason that I didn't hear the library door open. But she did. The next thing I knew I was flat on my back on the rug and she was draped across my chest kissing me.

And, as bad as that was, I managed to make it worse. Instead of grabbing her by the hair and yanking her off of me, I put an arm around her shoulders to pull her off of me and that was when Hamilton and Laura, coming out of the library, got their first look at us. It looked as if I was enjoying the proceedings as much as Cuba.

Then, when I finally did get her off of me, she contributed her bit towards making things worse.

"Oh, hello!" she leered up at Hamilton. "You two been having as much fun as we have?"

Hamilton looked the way I imagine a husband would look if he walked into his living room and found his wife casually sprawled out in front of the fire pawing the milkman.

There was just one good thing about it. So much anger, so much adrenalin, so much bile poured into his system that he reacted like a flooded motor. Instead of exploding into action, he went into shock, sort of. The hate and fury were still in his eyes but his voice came out icy and calm.

"No," he replied in answer to Cuba's question about having fun, "I'm afraid I've been boring Laura. She's terribly sleepy."

He even managed a little smile. Laura, who was still blushing over having caught Cuba and me, laughed nervously and said he hadn't bored her at all; she'd enjoyed every minute of it. "It was all that fresh air today. I can hardly keep my eyes open."

I got to my feet and said I thought I'd better be going up too; I was awfully tired myself. Hamilton looked at me so viciously that I almost explained to him that I wasn't bragging, I was complaining. The look Cuba gave me was just as nasty, but then she was purring:

"Well, sugar, aren't you going to help me up? You got me down here."

We made a real gay little group going up the stairs. Cuba and I led the way, with Laura and Hamilton bringing up the rear like a couple of wardens. At the top, Hamilton told Laura good night real sweetly, ignored Cuba and me and headed for his room towards the back of the house. Even rear-view, he looked mad. Laura prissed on ahead of us, went into her room and slammed the door. I glared at Cuba and told her I ought to throw her down the steps. She glared right back and said it would be just like me.

"You're a goddam beast, Farrell! We didn't *have* to come up. You just wait."

I ignored her until we got to my room and then I tried to reason with her again. I told her I wasn't playing hard to get; I just didn't want anything happening to her. "You've got that egomaniac mad enough to kill us both and if he gets back in that room by himself and gets to thinking about us being in a room together he just *might* kill us. Heat of passion. And he's really in heat."

Then I told her that if she would just wait until tomorrow, we would sneak down to Hamilton's boat. It had six bunks on it and we would spend the whole day christening them.

"No! *Tonight!*"

She swished on down the hall to her room. I went into my own room and Laura was standing at the bathroom door making a production out of her disgust.

"Oh, you're a great one, you are, Farrell. The man's not a killer, so you and Cuba are going to drive him to it."

I sighed, walked around to the side of the bed nearest her and sat down. I apologized for embarrassing her but told her that it wasn't my fault, it was Cuba's. "And don't get too mad at her because she's as much of a mental case as Hamilton."

I was serious. She was so full of herself she couldn't get along *with* men and so full of sex she couldn't get along without them either. I explained that to Laura. She was real touched.

"Oh, the poor, mixed-up little thing," she sneered.

I told her that she didn't know just how mixed up Cuba really was. "She's a mental soufflé. She's not content just to drive a man out of his mind, she wants to lock the door after him." I explained just what the set-up was: the arrogant way Hamilton had hired her and the fiendish way she was paying him back.

"Good God!" Laura gasped. "Pete, she can get you shot."

"And she can get you raped," I said, and I wasn't being a smart aleck saying it. "She's one of the reasons he is so hot after you. He wants to prove to her and himself that he can make love to a girl without paying her any five hundred dollars a week. That's the reason I worry when you go off with him. I know you're too nice to even let him kiss you but he's desperate."

I was afraid that might get her all huffy again but instead she smiled in such a way that I had the feeling she might think I was something besides a sex maniac. Then she confirmed it.

"Pete," she said, "if we weren't just old pals, I would kiss you for that." The smile turned into a grin. "John told me what you said you would do to him if he tried anything. He acted like he thought it was funny. I thought it was real sweet."

"Well, if you won't kiss me," I sighed, "will you listen to me for a couple of minutes?"

The grin faded but she said, all right. So I told her about seeing Jago in Cuba's room and why I thought Hamilton was so anxious about the journal. She sighed and gave me most of the same arguments that Cuba had. Then, I confronted her with what I had been about to confront Cuba with in front of the fire: the lousy trick that Hamilton had played on Ben Ponza by importing two of his ex-wives to meet his fiancée.

"Now, admit it!" I said. "Ben Ponza would never forgive a man for that, especially a man like Hamilton. He doesn't give a damn about what Hamilton's serials do for his circulation. He's been playing it cozy all this time just waiting for a clean shot at

Hamilton's throat and this is it. He knows something is about to pop in this Mary Belle thing and he wants us to get the story and pictures when it splatters on Hamilton."

Laura was back in her shell before I ever finished. "Good night, Pete," she said, starting to pull the bathroom door shut. "You're a sweet boy but a crazy boy."

"And you're the hardest-headed damn girl I ever saw!" The only answer I got was the bathroom door snapping shut in my face.

About two hours later I was in bed trying to get sound asleep. I'd dropped off into a light sleep about ten times but each time some weird dream had jerked me awake. Cuba and me making love in a sea of Lawdy Maudies and Hamilton and Jago shooting at us from the shore. Dreams like that.

Then I dreamed that Cuba was trying to get into the room. That really jerked me awake. I reached over and turned on the little lamp on the night table and looked over at the hall door. The chair I had propped under the knob was still in place. I lighted a cigarette, turned on the little transistor radio I had brought along and got an all-night station that was playing mood music. I turned it down low and switched off the lamp.

The music didn't help much. Outside, the wind was still rising, and inside were all the night noises you get in an old house but more of them than I ever heard. Our big, old house back in Stanton creaked and popped but Oakhurst could have furnished the sound track for a spook movie.

The chest of drawers would pop, a board in the floor would creak, somewhere a pipe in the wall would clank and out in the hall there would be a succession of creaks like somebody was creeping around.

Then, suddenly there was another noise that didn't belong in any repertoire of regular night noises. Somebody was opening the French door from the porch. Everything else was so eerie that Miss Maude's ghosts flashed through my mind. Then I had a worse thought: Cuba! But if she was coming she would have been there an hour ago, at least. Maybe it was Miss Maude. But what could she want? I put out my cigarette and eased down under the covers.

For about a half a minute I didn't hear a thing. Then I caught the damp, fresh smell of cold and rain. The door was already open and somebody or something was in the room. Then, a whisper in the darkness. "Pete?" It was Cuba. And she could wake up the whole house before I could hustle her out.

I started breathing heavy as though I was asleep. She hesitated, maybe because of the cigarette smoke and the music from the radio. Softly, she called out again. I breathed deeper and stirred a little. Then I heard her tiptoeing towards me. At the foot of the bed she paused. Then, instead of coming around the side of the bed as I had expected, she tiptoed on across the room. That's when I began to wonder just what the hell was going on.

I heard her ease the closet door open. She paused to listen. There was a click of a lock and then a thin line of light showed under the door. She was *in* the closet with the light on. I rolled over on my side to watch. The closet had my clothes hanging in it, some of my equipment, blankets, and a bunch of boxes with old clothes, curtains, etc., in them.

After about two minutes, maybe, the light went out. I heard the door creak open again and she was tiptoeing back towards the bed. Then she stopped and started whispering my name, this time a little louder. She wanted to wake me up now "Pete!" I stirred, groaned a little and gave a confused "Hunh?"

"It's Cuba," she whispered. "Turn on your light."

Hamilton, or no Hamilton, I decided to risk it. I had to find out what she had been doing in that closet. Still acting confused and sleepy, I sat up, reached over, turned on the lamp and then, nearly jumped clean out of my pajamas. Cuba, instead of being in a slinky black nightgown like I had figured, was covered from her neck to her toes in a fancy green velvet outfit that must have been all the rage back in 1850.

"What in the hell have you got on?" I wheezed.

"Oh, just a few little things that some of the Hamiltons left in my room and your closet," she smiled. "Since I was coming calling, I thought I should dress for the occasion."

It didn't make sense. For the kind of call she was making, she shouldn't have worn anything but knee pads. But she even had on a little green hat with a long white plume. Then, it did make sense. She evidently had figured that if she wore a slinky negligee, it would seem like the same old song, second verse; but by making it Novelty Night, I would be too intrigued to think about Hamilton.

I just stared at her. Her face took on this dreamy look, she put her hands to her hips, then, slowly, as though she was moving to the rhythm of the music, she brought them upwards along her waist and over her breasts and then she was slowly removing the little jacket to the dress. I knew what was coming and, despite the fact that I had seen the end result before, I could already feel myself slipping into a hypnotic state. She was going to torture me with an ante-bellum striptease.

The jacket dropped softly to the floor, the little hat with the big plume landed in a chair; then her fingers were at her throat freeing the fat little green velvet buttons from their loops. Down her front the fingers worked. At her waist they stopped and then they were at her throat again, slowly parting the dress.

Her shoulders went back, her breasts thrust forward, her arms, like ivory serpents, came out of the long green sleeves; then a wiggle of hips, a dainty disengagement about the ankles and there she was in nothing but the longest, damnedest looking slip I ever saw on a woman.

It came off. Then a shorter one, then one shorter than that. I thought I heard drums. It was the blood pounding in my ears. It was pounding out a message: "To hell with Hamilton! To hell with Hamilton! This is what you came for!" By that time she was down to her bra, panties—no stockings—and shiny red spike-heel shoes. My eyeballs felt like balloons.

When the bra dropped to the floor, I was vaguely aware of unbuttoning my pajama top. The pajama bottoms slid off with the panties. Then, she was out of the red shoes, onto the white sheets and in my arms.

She was the most frantic, the most passionate, but at the same time the most grateful girl it had ever been my pleasure to do business with. She moaned such endearing little things, made me feel so much like the world's greatest lover that I became a better Christian for it. Instead of getting in a big rush to gratify the excruciating hunger that had been gnawing at my vitals for weeks, I dedicated myself to gratifying hers first.

But then my public-spiritedness, my selflessness began to ebb and my own hunger began making demands. Things began getting out of control. Cuba's arms tightened around my neck. She began saying those endearing little things again. We were on the glory road! She completed the trip …. For me it was, at one and the same time, the most rapturous, the most frustrating, the most soul-sickening journey to the brink of ecstasy that a man ever took.

One second, I was entering another world, a world of almost unendurable delight. The next second that world was shattered—by a scream so full of terror that it pierced even my love-drugged brain. It came from Laura's room. Then she was pounding on the bathroom door.

"Pete! *Pete!*"

CHAPTER FIVE

Well, what do you do? You've got one beautiful girl in your arms and another one trying to tear your bathroom door down to get at you. My spirit wanted me to go to that door but my flesh wouldn't let me—despite the fact that Cuba was gyrating like a snake-goddess and hissing for me to turn her loose. I did the only thing I could.

"Laura, honey," I called out, "what's the matter?"

"The ghost!" she screamed. "Pete, I saw the ghost!"

That was a big relief. If she'd seen a burglar or a sex maniac, I would have rushed right in and laid down my life in her defense but a ghost never hurt anybody.

"Laura," I said, "you just had a nightmare, sugar. When you see something live, call me back."

Cuba hit me in the mouth with her elbow. "Damn you," she whispered. "Turn me loose and go to that door."

I turned her loose. "But don't you move," I snarled. "I'll be right back."

I got halfway to the door and she started snapping at me again. "Your pajamas, stupid!"

I'd forgotten 'em. With Laura still banging on the door and screaming, I grabbed 'em off the bed and put them on—wrong-side out but I didn't notice it at the time. Then I rushed over to the door, opened up, closed it behind me, and Laura threw herself in my arms.

"Oh, Pete, it was horrible! She was right by my bed."

It was typical Farrell luck. She was clinging to me like a baby squirrel to a high tree and didn't have a thing on but a little frilly, short-type nightgown and some little panty-type things, but she was trembling so that I couldn't feel anything but sorry for her.

"Sugar," I said, trying to console her and herd her back into her room at the same time. "You just had an old nightmare. Now …"

She balked on me. I was in her room and had her by the hand trying to pull her out of the bathroom but she didn't want any part of it.

"No! I'm not going back in there. That girl was standing right by my …"

It was her turn to be interrupted. The door out into the hall flew open and in flew Miss Maude and Hamilton. Miss Maude looked like she had just escaped from a beauty shop fire: hair in curlers, grease all over her face and one of those chin hammocks for her jowls.

As for Hamilton, everything about him—silk pajamas, silk robe, fancy slippers—was elegant except his manner. He saw me pulling at Laura, saw my pajamas wrong side out, saw the wild, frustrated look in my eyes and bellowed:

"For God's sake, Farrell! Wasn't raping my secretary enough? Must you start on the guests?"

I turned Laura loose and turned on him. "One more word," I said, "and I start on you."

"*What* are you doing in this room?"

"Trying to get her out of my room!" I snapped. I wasn't so mad that I wasn't thinking. I wanted to get the fact that she had come to my room on record. "She thinks she saw Mary Belle. She had a nightmare."

"It wasn't a nightmare!" Laura said. "I saw her. She was right there."

She pointed to a spot in between the two big old beds and Hamilton stopped snarling at me and started snarling at Miss Maude.

"I *hope* you're satisfied."

Miss Maude ignored him and crossed the room beaming at Laura.

"You poor child. But wasn't it exciting, dear? I told you it was a grand night for her to be walking. Was she wearing blue again?"

It was the damnedest conversation I ever heard. I knew women were nuts about clothes but I never knew they would talk about clothes on a ghost.

Laura said she wasn't positive just what color she was wearing because Mary Bell's face was the only thing she got a good look at, but she had the feeling that she was wearing something pink and old-fashioned. Miss Maude made some comment that I ignored because I was beginning to feel womanish, too—like a woman who's got a chicken just about done in the oven and then people come to call.

So, I interrupted Hamilton, who was calling Miss Maude an idiot, and said:

"Now, we all know it was just a nightmare so why don't we all go back to our rooms and get some sleep?"

Well, I hadn't any more gotten that out when in strolled my chicken, good old Cuba. She had returned to her room by the porch route and then come back down the hall. She had on a filmy pink gown and a filmy pink negligee but neither one of them was as filmy as the look on her face.

"Why, what in the world is this all about?" she asked.

She was acting so innocent that Hamilton automatically figured she was guilty of something. In the split second he took to think it over, Laura said real defiantly:

"I saw the ghost. I saw Mary Belle."

Cuba cut her eyes at me and for a second I thought she was going to laugh at all the weird things that happened to wreck my love life but then she was all sympathy.

"Well, welcome to the club. I don't blame you for screaming. And she'll be back. The first night I saw her she came back and ran her hand over my face. Oh, it was ghastly."

I wanted to kill her and so did Hamilton.

"Goddammit!" he snapped. "Now, stop that. It was nothing but a nightmare."

"So let's everybody get back to bed," I said, cutting my eyes at Cuba.

"*No!*" Laura said. "I'm not staying in this room and having that girl run her hand over my face."

"Don't you know Cuba's kidding you?" I said. "Now, everybody back to bed."

I don't know whether it was my hurry or the amused look in Cuba's eyes that did it but Hamilton got this steely, knowing expression on his face.

"No," he said, taking a fatherly turn. "Even if it was a nightmare, I can understand Laura's being upset." He turned to Cuba. "I'm sure you wouldn't mind spending the rest of the night here. There's the other bed for you."

I almost gasped out loud because I sure hadn't lived through the winter to die in the spring.

"That's the most ridiculous thing I ever heard of," I said, stepping between him and Laura. "Why, if it ever got back to *Chic* magazine that somebody had to sleep with Laura Ames because she thought she saw a ghost she'd be laughed clean off the staff."

For a second I thought I had gotten away with it but then Laura shoved me out of the way.

"He's crazy!" she snapped. "When I tell them what happened they'll give me a medal for not swimming back to the mainland right now. You're darn right I want her to stay in here with me. Nobody's running their clammy, dead fingers over *my* face."

It was my turn to get indignant.

"Haven't you got *any* shame? A twenty-five-year-old girl having to have somebody …"

"Twenty-*four!*" she said. "And if I was a hundred and twenty-four it still wouldn't …" She stopped and looked at Cuba. "Why don't I sleep in your room?"

"Now, you're making sense," I said. "You sleep in Cuba's room and Cuba sleeps in here." I glared at Cuba. "She doesn't mind hands running over her face and …"

"There is only one bed in Cuba's room," Hamilton said, still not knowing why he was fighting me except that if I was for it, he was against it. "There are two beds here and Cuba won't mind a bit."

I wanted to choke him. "Just what is this?" I said, looking more indignant than ever. "You *know* that Cuba's trying to scare Laura. It'd be just like her to put a sheet over her head when Laura gets to sleep and I'll be damned if I'm going to be wakened out of a sound sleep again with all that shrieking and pounding on my …"

Cuba started laughing.

"Laura, he's teasing." She winked at her and then smiled at Miss Maude and Hamilton. "I'll stay. We'll be fine."

"But I'm right in the next room," I said.

"Don't remind us of it," Hamilton said.

Cuba gave me this leering smile. "I'll call you if I need you."

I couldn't believe it. She knew good and well why I had been putting up such a fight to keep her away from Laura. I had been real nice and sweet to her and she was going to spend the rest of the night in my bed being real nice and sweet to me.

"I'll check on you," I said.

"Don't bother," Hamilton smirked. "I'm sure Cuba can handle everything."

"Why don't you go to bed?" I snarled.

"Yes, dear," Miss Maude said. "I'm sure everything's going to be fine now." She smiled at Laura. "I'm so glad you saw her, dear, but don't you worry about her any more. When she walks this late she usually doesn't come back."

With that Hamilton nodded real belligerently, gave Cuba and me a last glare and then put his arm around Miss Maude and herded her out of the room. I just kept standing there.

"*Well?*" Laura snapped.

I glared at Cuba.

"Would you step into the bathroom just a minute? I want to have a few words with you."

I just wanted to make certain that she understood the situation, that she wasn't under any impression that she had discharged her obligations to me or that I was just wishing her sweet dreams. Laura had to butt in, though.

"Pete, I don't think Cuba is in the habit of meeting men in bathrooms. I'm sure that anything you have to say to her you can say in front of me."

She was already getting stuffy because of the fool she'd made of herself and Cuba capitalized on it.

"Sure," she smirked. "What do you want to tell me?"

I almost blurted it out. I almost told her that I wanted her to get the hell back in my bed where she had been putting on that rodeo about ten minutes before. But I was too much of a gentleman and she knew it. So I turned on Laura instead.

"Haven't you caused enough trouble?"

"*Well,*" she said, getting real haughty, "I'll know who to go to for help next time."

She meant Hamilton and that was supposed to crush me but it didn't.

"It's too late for that," I said. "You've had it. You thought you saw a ghost and you came banging on my door for help."

She tried to look blank.

"Now what's that supposed to mean?"

I stared at the two of them and gave a long, drawn-out bitter sigh. Two gorgeous women, one of 'em knowing that I was too much of a gentleman to say that she had just been in bed with me and the other one knowing that I was too much of a gentleman to say that we had made a bargain about a ghost and about her banging on my door for help and that, now, by the terms of that bargain she belonged to me body and soul.

"By God, you're *both* going to pay for this!" I snarled. I grabbed the bathroom door and started swinging it shut. "And don't think I'm going to forget it."

I slammed the door and didn't even put my ear to it to hear what they were saying about me. I knew that I would hear both of them saying that they didn't have any idea what I was talking about and then I would have been forced to go back in and spell it out for them.

So, I went back into my room, poured myself a glassful of whiskey, got in bed and started nursing it. But I still couldn't believe what had happened. No girl, not even Cuba, could be this fiendish to a boy who had been so nice to her. If she had one spark of indecency left in her, she would come sneaking back into my room.

Two hours later I was thrashing around in my bed cursing, smoking, nursing the bottle and still telling myself that. Finally, I couldn't stand it any longer. I crept into the bathroom, cracked the door to Laura's room and started cursing again. They were both sleeping so peacefully and innocently the place sounded like an angel roost.

I eased into the room and started creeping around to Cuba's bed. I was going to wake her up. Halfway there, Laura started moaning in her sleep. That slowed me down. Then I had a thought that stopped me cold.

If Cuba was bitchy enough to go to sleep on me without coming back to my room, she would sure be bitchy enough to scream when I woke her up. Maybe she wasn't even asleep. Maybe she was lying there faking that deep breathing and waiting to scare hell out of me when I started shaking her foot. That, in turn, would scare the hell out of Laura and the house would be in an uproar again.

I went back to my room … still with one consolation. Laura, by our bargain, was mine, and as mad as I was I sure wasn't going to have any pangs about collecting.

Around seven the next morning I felt even stronger about it. She came banging on the door and woke me up to one of those hangovers that make you feel like you've got an ice pick in your ears.

"Pete," she called out, "I'm going deer hunting with John."

Just like that. No mention of any night of terror, no thanking me for rescuing her from a ghost. Instead, she wakes me up just to tell me she's going off with a sex maniac I've warned her about.

"Fine," I growled. "Take Mary Belle with you."

She ignored that completely. "Cuba's going riding, I think," she said. "Why don't you go with her?"

I shuddered. She couldn't help knowing how my head would feel aboard a horse. I told her, no, thanks, but for her and Cuba to take good care of themselves.

"I got big plans for you two fiends."

"Now, what's that supposed to mean?" she snapped.

"I'll tell you tonight," I said.

I slept until around nine and then went down and ate breakfast with Miss Maude. She was having whiskey in her coffee or vice versa and talked the whole time. First, there was some stuff about Laura and the ghost; then she briefed me on the day up to then. She hadn't found her journal, Jago was sick in bed with a bug of some sort; the northeaster had slacked off but would be kicking up again and John, Laura and Cuba were fools to be out in it.

She finally talked me clean out of the house with my head still feeling like a tambourine. I told her that I thought a little fresh air would do me good and that I was going to take a little walk down to the beach.

"Now, remember yesterday, Peter," she smiled, wagging a finger at me. "You stay out of trouble this time."

It was uncanny. Before I had gone ten feet down that driveway I was in trouble again. It started with one of my shoelaces working loose. I knelt to tie it and as I did I noticed beside my foot the fresh imprint of a horse's hoof. Right away my instinct for disaster started asserting itself. This voice within me said:

Farrell, the rider of that horse is that sexual vampire who feasted on your life's blood last night. Why don't you track the fiendish bitch down and make her restore your soul?

Off I went.

I tracked her down the driveway to the right. As I did, this other voice tried making itself heard. The voice of reason.

Farrell, she's probably got a riding crop. You try dragging her off that horse and she'll put so many stripes on you, you'll look like a zebra.

Naturally, I didn't listen to that voice. She'd put welts on my soul; a body to match wouldn't make any difference. Halfway around the driveway she had turned down the beach road to the right, the road I had come up the day before in the bathing suit. Then, about a hundred yards further on, I really got hooked. She had turned the horse off the road into the woods on the left.

Why had she done it? She was a maniac, of course, but that was beside the point. Why make a gray, soggy day even more miserable by turning off a road to ride through a bunch of dripping trees and wet bushes?

It didn't make sense. And, with my weakness for things that didn't make sense, I followed her into the trees and the bushes. She started bearing to the left. The next thing I knew I had come out on the road that we had taken the day before to her favorite spot on the beach. That didn't make sense either. Why hadn't she come down the road directly from the house instead of cutting back to it through the woods?

I kept following the tracks … over the creek bridge, past the cemetery, then the road forked. One fork led on down the island, the other to the dock. She had taken the one to the dock. When I saw that I started cursing myself.

That dear, sweet girl had remembered what I'd said about the spend-the-day picnic and orgy aboard Hamilton's boat. She had known I would follow her, she had chosen such a devious route to fool the others and now she was aboard awaiting me with open arms and a full head of steam.

I walked in that Fool's Paradise until I was about a hundred yards from the dock. I could see it and the marsh at the end of the tunnel of trees. And to the left of the dock, tied to a bush, was Cuba's horse. She *was* on the boat. I broke into a trot. Then I saw something else. Coming up the ladder alongside the dock was Jago.

Automatically I stopped and edged over into the bushes alongside the road. What the hell was he doing at the dock? Miss Maude had told me at breakfast that he was sick in bed. The only thing I could see wrong with him was his nerves. He looked out at the marsh, looked all around at the woods, peered down the road, hurried over to Cuba's horse, untied it and led it into the woods. Then I heard him tramping off, evidently headed back to the house.

For about five minutes I didn't make a move. Just what the hell *was* going on? The most horrible thought I had was that Cuba had come down to play house with Jago. But even he wasn't monster enough to make love to a woman and then steal her horse. And why hadn't he ridden the horse back to the house? Why walk it off into the woods?

After I was positive that he wasn't coming back, I sneaked my way down through the bushes to the dock and looked out at the boat. It was a plush forty-foot cruiser with lots of mahogany and brass, riding at storm anchor out in the middle of the creek that ran through the marsh from the bay. But there wasn't any sign of life. I edged out onto the dock.

"Cuba!" I hollered.

No answer. A ridiculous thought hit me. Maybe I hadn't been following Cuba's horse, maybe it was Jago's. He had just come down to check the boat maybe and had taken a short-cut back. But why that crazy route he had taken and what about that business of him being sick?

I hollered for Cuba again. Then I eased down the ladder into the dinghy, rowed out and climbed aboard the cruiser. It reminded me of a sea movie, the scene where the captain and the mate climb aboard a ghost ship and the captain gives this ominous sniff and says he can just *smell* trouble aboard her.

"Cuba!" I shouted.

Still no answer. I went below and checked the aft cabins and the galley. Still no Cuba. Then, the forward cabin. There she was stretched out on a bunk. She had met Jago all right but it hadn't been on purpose.

She was tied up, beat up and knocked out!

CHAPTER SIX

When I was twelve years old, my fat cousin, Buster Farrell, and I were riding a mule double across a rickety, old bridge. Halfway across, the flooring to the bridge caved in, and me and Buster and the mule fell fifteen feet into the creek. When the mule wasn't kicking me, Buster, who couldn't swim too good, was trying to climb on my head. After that I never had any fear of water because I knew the Lord didn't mean for me to die by drowning.

So, after I got poor Cuba attended to, I pulled in the anchors, hoisted the dinghy into the cockpit, climbed up to the flying bridge and, a couple of minutes later, started easing down the creek. The wind was rising again and the bay looked like something that Moses wouldn't try crossing. I gunned her, asked the Lord to remember Buster and the mule, and held on.

At times I was bouncing so that I felt like the whole boat was a pogo stick; at other times I felt like it was a submarine, but twenty minutes later I was across the bay and bucking my way up the Caloosa River towards the Queensport docks. All the commercial fishermen were there battening down their boats for the storm and when I pulled alongside, Harney Stokes, the man I had hoped would be around, jumped aboard. He was wearing black, foul-weather gear and a slack mouth.

"You lost your damn mind?" he hollered above the wind. "You come across that bay?"

"I came *through* it!" I shouted down from the bridge. "Now, where's a doctor? I got to get to one without anybody but us knowing it."

He stared up at me. "By God, you need a doctor. A *head* doctor. Now, cut that engine and let's get this thing tied up."

He grabbed a line and started to jump back onto the dock but I stopped him. "Don't do that if you ever want to find out what happened to Mary Belle," I said. "Stay on here."

He stopped, stared at me again, and then turned and stared at the boys on the dock to see if any of them had heard me. They hadn't.

"What about Mary Belle?"

"Get me to that doctor," I said.

He hesitated as though debating whether to ship aboard with a maniac or not. "Take her back downriver. Down to Doc Bagshaw's place."

I came around and he started climbing up to the bridge.

"Now, what in hell is this all about?"

"Just check that forward cabin," I said. "That'll give you a hint."

Knowing that I was getting even with him for the lockjaw treatment he had given me when I asked *him* about Mary Belle, he just glared at me and turned back and went below. I had Cuba wrapped in a blanket but she was still out cold. Jago had hit her with something on the back of the head and raised a knot big enough to be a goiter of the skull.

A minute or so later, Harney climbed up on the bridge and, with me feeling like a sea-going St. Bernard, said:

"Goddam, Farrell, you didn't finally have to knock her in the head to get it, did you?"

I started to slug him. I save a girl's life but instead of getting a Carnegie medal, I get a morals charge thrown at me.

"Thanks," I sneered. "But Jago hit her."

"Jago?" he wheezed. "By God, yesterday she's wrestling you, today she's fighting Jago. Just what the hell is going on over on that island? And what the hell's it got to do with Mary Belle?"

"Take the wheel," I sighed.

He took it. I braced myself in the companion seat alongside him and told him about my tracking Cuba and then finding her in Jago's wake on the boat.

"But," I wound up, "I know now that Cuba didn't come down to this boat for any hanky-panky with me. She came down here to do something else. Whatever it was, Hamilton must have suspected she would try it and had Jago lying in wait for her—with orders to kill her if she tried it"

He shook his head. "Well, why didn't he kill her?"

I had to admit I didn't know.

"But he had her tied up. He must have been figuring on coming back and then killing her."

"So it would seem," Harney said, "but there must've been something more on his mind than just killing her. How in hell they figure on getting away with it?"

I told him I didn't know that either.

"But one thing I do know," I said. "This thing has got to do with Mary Belle. Hamilton wouldn't risk murder on the installment plan like this unless it was to cover up another murder, Mary Belle's murder; now, would he?"

He started stalling. "How you know it's Hamilton? Maybe Jago was down checking the boat like you thought at first and this girl comes along and ..."

"And he rapes his boss's secretary and then *leaves* her tied up? What do you think he is? Some sort of sexual pack-rat? Gonna keep her stashed away? You know he did it on Hamilton's orders and you know it's got something to do with Mary Belle. Now, what do you think it is?"

Harney switched jaws with his chew of tobacco and kept peering out at the river. "I'll tell you what I think when you tell me how much you know about Mary Belle."

I told him I didn't *know* anything because all my information had come from either a bunch of sneaky, bad-mouthed fishermen or lying women.

"But I got theories," I snapped.

"Who ain't?" he grunted. "What's yores?"

I told him: Mary Belle was pregnant, she was giving Hamilton trouble and when the hurricane came along he saw his chance, killed her and sank her body some place.

"I don't think she ever reached that boat alive despite what Miss Maude says."

"Well," Harney sighed, "now, I'll tell you what I think about this whole thing. I think you've screwed it up to a fare-thee-damn-well."

"Gee, thanks," I said. "The next time I see a girl with her head bashed in I'll leave her for seed."

"It ain't that," he said, and then proceeded to tell me what it was.

He said that everybody else in Queensport had had the same notions about Mary Belle that I did, everybody that is except Tom Gill, the county chief of police. He had seemed to accept Hamilton's story of Mary Belle's boat swamping.

So Harney and a few other civic leaders decided they would pay Hamilton a little visit and see if he would tell the same story with a rope around his neck. Right away, Tom Gill called a secret meeting.

He told Harney and his neck-stretchers that the police, the State Police included, thought Hamilton was guilty, too, and they had laid a trap for him. But for him to take the bait, he would have to keep on thinking that he had gotten away with murder.

"So we put the rope away," Harney said. "But Tom still wouldn't tell us what the trap was. He was scared somebody might talk but I think we know what the bait in the trap was now, don't we, Farrell?"

He shook his head at me.

"It was this girl, Cuba. She was working with the police but you had to go over there with them hot pants and ..."

"Now, just one damn second," I said. I realized there wouldn't be anything easier to plant on Hamilton than a sexy secretary but there was still one big thing wrong.

"If Cuba was an undercover agent," I said, "why didn't she get under the cover with him? You can't make a man shoot off his mouth giving him that hot tongue and cold shoulder treatment that she did."

That stopped him for a second and he shifted his cud again. "Well, she must have been working on Miss Maude, then. The way she gets liquored up all the time, the police maybe figured she'd let something slip to Cuba about what happened the day Mary Belle disappeared."

The police, he explained, didn't think that Miss Maude knew anything about the murder but they did think that she was so sold on her dear brother being innocent that she had furnished him with the alibi about seeing Mary Belle off at the dock. My thoughts had been along that line, too, but Harney still wasn't giving me credit for being any brain. He peered out at a channel marker up ahead and started easing the boat in towards the left shore.

"Now, just what did you do over there with yore tomcatting that tipped Hamilton off to this girl?"

"Nothing!" I snapped. I had been thinking about that too, but I was innocent. "I helped get him mad at her but it didn't have a thing to do with Mary Belle."

"Must have," he said. "You just didn't realize it. You talk to her about Mary Belle?"

"Yeah, and she just laughed at me," I said. "And Hamilton wasn't around to hear me asking her. At least not the afternoon I was going to get Miss Maude drunk."

Harney groaned. "I s'pose you were gonna get that po', innocent, old woman lap-legged and make her tell you all about Mary Belle. How soon before she passed you out?"

I got a little offended at that.

"Not before she admitted to me that she had been keeping a journal that Hamilton didn't know about. It was all about the storm and ..."

I stopped and Harney semed to sense why. That damn journal could explain everything.

"What journal?" Harney asked.

Things started falling into place. "The journal that Miss Maude couldn't find. And I think the reason she couldn't find it is that Cuba must have it. Or had it."

Harney nodded. "I still don't know what you're talking about but it makes more sense than anything else you've said. Say it again."

I took it from the top. First, I explained to him the potential of the journal, how Miss Maude might have innocently put something in it that would wreck Hamilton's story of what had happened the day of the storm. Then I explained how Cuba could have come into possession of it.

She had been in the library that afternoon and, as loud as Miss Maude and I had been talking, she couldn't have helped but hear us talking about the journal. Being sober and being tied in with the police, she could have figured it was a lead and, while Miss Maude and I were belting down Lawdy Maudies, gone up and gotten it.

"And there must have been something in it that made her decide she'd better get to the police with it as soon as she could. The boat was the only way she could do it."

Harney agreed that it made sense ... *if* we were right about Cuba working for the police.

"But we still don't know how Hamilton come to suspect her."

I sighed. "He probably figured that I wasn't interested in anything but sex and whiskey but he knew from the way Cuba had treated him that she wasn't primarily interested in that. So, if anybody had got the journal it was her. So he had Jago lying in wait for her on the boat just in case he was right."

"And she must have figured you wouldn't be any help or she would've come to you?"

I didn't bother going into the implications of that.

"You don't know just how fiendish that girl is," I snapped. "She probably wanted to pull the job off all by herself and make fools out of Hamilton and me both."

He must have decided there wasn't any more future in insulting me. "All right," he said, "if she is with the police and she did get that journal, where is it?"

That was a real good question. I told him we wouldn't know for sure until she regained consciousness.

"And then," he snarled, heading in towards shore, "me and Tom Gill and the boys are gonna pay him a visit."

I stared at him. "And just what the hell will that accomplish?"

If she had had the journal with her, then Jago had stuck it in his shirt and gone back to the house with it. If she had hidden it around the house instead, then Hamilton and Jago could have found it and burned it.

"And if you haven't got the journal," I concluded, "you haven't got any proof—at least proof that will stand up against Mary Belle's murderers. All you've got is an assault and battery case against Jago and he can say she just shook that pretty fanny of hers in his face and he went berserk. And I'll have to testify that the thing was enough to make any man go berserk."

"Then just what do you suggest?" Harney sneered. "Sitting on our butts and letting Tom Gill book you for boat stealing and body snatching?"

"You're just gonna sit and I'm gonna take the boat back," I said.

"By God, you *have* lost your mind. You been lucky enough getting this boat across that bay once. If you ..." He stared at me. "Suppose you did get it back across?"

"Well, if I'm lucky," I said, "they won't know I've been gone. Jago's back playing sick in his room, Hamilton's off in the woods deer hunting with another girl and I'm supposed to be taking a walk on the beach.

"When Jago comes down to finish off Cuba or whatever he's going to do with her, he'll find her gone. They'll think she's gotten loose, couldn't run the boat or something and tried to escape in the dinghy, which I'll set loose in the creek when I get back. They'll find it, think she has taken to the woods on the island and is hiding or trying to hail a boat.

"Hamilton will either go nuts hunting for her or he may crack under the strain and do something that will throw some light on Mary Belle. And all that time you'll have Cuba here with the doctor and Tom Gill. I'll be over there watching those two slippery sonsofbitches."

Harney nodded slowly and then looked out at the weather.

"Just a couple of things wrong with that," he drawled. "This wind is really gonna start blowing in a while and you could be cut off over there for two whole days maybe and we couldn't get to you."

He throttled down and headed the boat towards a small dock jutting out from some live oaks along the bank.

"And the other thing is this," he added. "If you don't get back before them slippery sonsofbitches discover you're gone, we might just wind up hunting for you and Mary Belle *both*."

CHAPTER SEVEN

A n hour or so later I was back on Spanish Point sloshing up the beach road through a rain heavy enough to strangle frogs. But it suited my dark purposes fine. Any tracks I might have made around the dock and other such incriminating places would be washed out. So, except for being worn out, hung-over, half-drowned and still a little seasick, I was pretty happy. Cuba was taken care of, Hamilton's boat was taken care of and pretty soon I hoped to have him accommodated, too.

And just like I figured, he had been awfully concerned about me during my absence. Turning into the driveway, I saw him on the porch peering out into the storm like an anxious mother. I knew just what was going through his diseased mind: had I been out just catching cold or had I blundered across Cuba and caught him cold? When he saw me coming from the road to the beach instead of the one to the boat, he figured everything was all right and reverted to form.

"My God, Farrell," he called out, "I thought you at least had sense enough to come in out of the rain."

"I'd rather be wet by myself than dry with some lousy writer," I hollered back. It wasn't very good but it sounded normal for me and that's the way I wanted him to think things were—normal.

"Well, hurry up and get changed," he said, as I splashed up the steps. "We're waiting lunch on you and Cuba."

I looked appropriately surprised.

"Cuba's still out in this slop?"

"Yes, our *other* problem child is still out," he said, ushering me into the house. "Probably in the shack at the other end of the island waiting for the rain to let up. She'll be along."

Miss Maude came out of the living room and said that she certainly hoped he was right. Then she got a good look at me and said that anybody as wet as I was on the outside had no business being dry on the inside, wouldn't I like a drink to take up with me. I begged off and went on up.

Laura was in her room. I knocked on her bathroom door knowing what sort of reception I would get. She was going to be real snippity. Not only had I rescued her from a "ghost"—something no woman can ever forgive you for—I'd made that mysterious threat about having plans for her. She opened up, saw that I looked like something the dogs had been chasing, and really got snippity.

"Well, Farrell," she leered, "what did you do to Cuba this time?"

"Oh, nothing much," I said, swaggering into her room with the water still squirting from my shoes. "I just saved her life."

"How nice," she said, and turned her back on me and headed for her dresser. "Especially since you had plans for her."

"Well, I'm afraid she's not in any shape for what I had in mind," I said. "Guess you'll have to carry on for the two of you."

She acted like she didn't have any idea what I was talking about and kept looking in the mirror messing with her hair. "Farrell, did Cuba come in with you? Miss Maude's beginning to worry about her."

"No, she didn't come in with me," I said real matter-of-factly. "She's over in Queensport at the doctor's."

In the mirror I saw her start to give a big sigh of disgust but then she saw the way I was looking and checked it. She turned from the mirror and faced me.

"Farrell, just how much have you had to drink this morning?"

"About eighty gallons," I said. "All of it sea water. Swallowed it taking Cuba over to Queensport."

"What *are* you talking about?" she snapped. "Has something happened to Cuba?"

"Yeah," I said, and then gave her the nastiest smile I could muster. "You see how it is when somebody knows something and keeps toying with you about it?"

She didn't even have the decency to blush. "Nobody's been toying with you. Now what happened to Cuba?"

"Jago waylaid her on Hamilton's boat and then knocked her out and tied her up," I said. "At Hamilton's orders."

She started to blurt out something, then just stared at me.

"I'm giving you one more chance," I said. "Ben Ponza did send us down here about Mary Belle's murder, didn't he?"

"So *that's* it," she snapped. "You come in here with this perfectly fantastic story trying to bluff me into telling you something I know absolutely *nothing* about."

That was that. I'd given her a chance to show me some mercy and get herself off the hook. She hadn't taken it, so anything I did to her thereafter would be justified.

"Sit down!" I growled.

I plopped her down into a chair and told her everything that had happened that morning and everything I had been told, especially about Tom Gill and the State Police. Then I really got worked up. I started pacing up and down in front of the chair shaking my finger at her.

"And you and Ben Ponza *knew* the police were working on this case," I said, "and you knew what you were getting me into. Well, you got me into it and I'm getting myself out of it even if it means breaking your pretty neck along with Jago's and Hamilton's. Now you just march downstairs and start acting like hasn't anything happened. But when I tell you to do something, you do it and you do it quick, you hear me?"

It was quite a speech. The first part of it, when I was telling her about finding Cuba, she started getting scared but the last part of it, when I was telling her that I was taking over, she started getting indignant. Which was what I wanted. Better an indignant woman than a scared one.

"Pete Farrell," she snapped, "I don't believe a word you're saying. John Hamilton wouldn't be that stupid. How could he expect to get away with it and ..."

"You believe every word I'm saying," I said, "and if you want to find out how he expects to get away with it and if you want to find out what happened to Mary Belle and if you want to get out of this alive, you'd better do exactly what I say and do it when I say it."

I left her mad enough to claw me and went in and took a hot shower and got cleaned up. When I went back downstairs they were all in the parlor having a drink. Laura gave me a look you could use to shrink heads and then went back to laughing at Hamilton.

He was talking about their hunt that morning and joking about how she had seen four deer, had shot nine times and hadn't scorched a hair. Miss Maude shoved a drink at me and told Laura she shouldn't feel badly at all.

"At least, dear, you didn't nearly kill someone," she said, settling down in a chair and smiling. "My first hunt I nearly bagged my father."

Laura laughed. "Your father?"

"I really did," Miss Maude said. "He was coming to get me off my stand and I mistook him for a deer coming through the brush, and shot. If I had been any sort of marksman at all he would have wound up over the mantel. For some reason he never took me hunting again."

Everybody laughed at that except me. I wanted to laugh but my throat had suddenly gone dry. Miss Maude, bless her gabby old soul, had given me what I thought was the answer to my mystery. I looked over at Hamilton. He was still smiling but instead of looking at Laura, as he had been doing, he was looking down at his drink, studying it.

I took a deep breath and started in. "Well, what sort of shoulder-buster did you have Laura shooting, Hamilton? An elephant gun?"

He didn't take offense at all because he saw the way Laura glared at me. That's the way he wanted it: trusting him and sore at me.

"Sweetest, lightest, little deer rifle you ever saw," he smirked. "Had it made up especially for our lady guests so they would have no excuses."

They had another little laugh out of that. I followed my pattern. "Yeah?" I said. "Let me see it."

For just a split second that arrogant look in his eyes gave way to panic and I knew I was on the right track.

"Certainly, Mr. Farrell, you may see it," he said, regaining his composure. "But if you knew anything at all about fine guns I'm sure you would know that it is customary after having shot one, especially in the rain, to have it cleaned. I've taken it back to Jago and as soon as he cleans it you may have your look."

It was such a long, sweet, sickening speech that Miss Maude got up in the middle of it, went to the door, looked out and started wondering out loud where Cuba could be.

Hamilton, having quieted me, got to his feet and quieted her.

"Dear, I've told you that Cuba is probably in the shack at the end of the island waiting out the rain. And probably hoping that we are worrying about her which I can assure you I am not. Now, stop fretting."

Right then Mattie came in and asked if it would be all right to go ahead with lunch. Miss Maude told her to go ahead, and put Miss Cuba's up. Then she added a very innocent but very timely question.

"How's poor Jago?"

Mattie looked appropriately grateful for her mistress' concern.

"He's still sleeping, Miss Maude. I think when he wakes up he's gonna be all right. Just one of them bugs."

Lunch went as usual. Hamilton drooled over Laura and at the other end of the table Miss Maude and I boozed it up a little and talked about the journal that was still missing. Hamilton didn't even cut his eyes at her so I wondered if the thing *was* still missing.

After lunch I got a break. We went back into the parlor and Hamilton excused himself and went upstairs. Miss Maude took another long look out of the door for Cuba and then excused herself and went upstairs, too. I was on one of the settees thumbing through a magazine. When Miss Maude went up I looked up at Laura standing in front of the big fireplace. She had started glaring at me again. Then she came over and plopped down beside me.

"Pete Farrell," she said in a low, vicious voice, "you *were* lying. If what you said about Cuba was so, Hamilton couldn't be acting the way he has."

"How's he been acting," I drawled, beginning to thumb through the magazine again.

"Hungry. He ate every bit of his lunch. If he knew there was a poor, beat-up girl somewhere he couldn't eat a bite. Nobody could. He's …"

She was interrupted by Miss Maude calling down the stairs and asking Mattie to come help her with something. Mattie, who was cleaning off the table, hollered that she was coming. She came through the parlor, went out into the front hall and started up the stairs. I sat there listening to her.

"What's the matter with you?" Laura whispered. She knew I had something in mind. As soon as I heard Mattie reach the top of the stairs I got to my feet.

"Come on. I'm gonna show you the healthiest sick man alive."

Before she could get her mouth into gear, I had hustled her through the dining room and kitchen and into the quarters that Jago and Mattie had off the kitchen. There was a little living room, a bath and a bedroom. By the time I pushed the bedroom door open, Laura had stopped sputtering enough to be coherent.

"Dammit, why do I want to see Jago?"

I relaxed my hold on her arm.

"There *ain't* any Jago."

It was just what I figured. There was a big, unmade, double-bed in the room but not a soul in it. Laura blinked. I made her feel the pillows and the sheets. They were stone cold.

"Just remember," I whispered. "There's not anybody in this bed and there hasn't been for at least a half an hour. Now, let's get out of here."

I closed everything up, hurried her back into the parlor off the dining room, sat her down on the settee and started thumbing through the magazine again. She glared at me and said, "All right, what's that supposed to mean?"

"Ask Ben Ponza," I said.

Before she could find anything to break over my head, Mattie came downstairs and started through the parlor. I looked up and asked her very sweetly if she would mind my coming back and taking a look at the rifle Jago had.

"The one Miss Laura used," I said. "Jago's been cleaning it. I want to see if it's as light as Mr. Hamilton said."

She stopped and stared at me, trying to figure out if I was as innocent as I sounded.

"But Jago's asleep," she said, as though that should explain everything.

"But I don't want to see Jago," I said, getting to my feet. "I just want to see the rifle. Couldn't you sneak it out of his room. I'll come back and …"

That panicked her. "Nossir! I ain't chancing waking him. Soon as he wakes up and cleans it, I'll show it to you."

With that she went into the dining room, grabbed the tray of dishes and disappeared into the kitchen.

I turned to Laura.

"You satisfied now? She knows he's not in that room and she knows the rifle's not either. Hamilton knows it too."

I had her but she didn't want to admit it. "How do you know that they know. Where *is* Jago?"

"I'm just guessing," I said, "but if my theory about this thing is right, Jago waited for me to come in for lunch, then got out of bed, grabbed that rifle, slipped out the back way and headed down to the boat to finish Cuba off. Right now I think he's on the boat wondering where in the hell she's gone."

Laura's eyes narrowed. She knew it was beginning to form a pattern but she still couldn't read the design.

"And now you think you know how they're going to try and pull this off."

I nodded and casually started thumbing through the magazine again, which had the desired effect. She got madder.

"And I'm supposed to sit here and beg you to explain it all to me."

"Either that," I said, "or you can try wiggling your way back into my good graces by telling me how right I was about Ben Ponza sending us here. Does he know anything about this that I don't already know?"

"No!" she snapped. And from her grim, pretty lips, there finally came the whole ugly story of my being had.

Ben had somehow gotten a tip that the police were working on the case. Laura and I—for *Chic*—were supposed to get pictures and background material of Hamilton on his home grounds. When the case broke—if it did—all the material would be turned over to *Probe,* the news magazine, and it would have the jump on everybody.

"But Ben had absolutely no idea that anything would happen," Laura added. "And to make certain that nothing happened he told me not to tell you what it was all about. He said that you were such a wild man, that if you did know anything about it, something *would* happen."

She stopped being apologetic and started sneering.

"And he was certainly right, wasn't he? If you hadn't tried raping Cuba, you wouldn't have met those fishermen and, if you hadn't met them, you wouldn't have made a fool of yourself trying to get Miss Maude drunk and, if you hadn't tried that, Cuba wouldn't have heard about the journal and, if ..."

I interrupted to ask if she couldn't show a little more respect for the man in charge. That stopped her.

"All right, dammit," she said. "I've told you about Ben, now you tell me about Hamilton. What's he going to do? What's going to happen?"

"Well, the next thing that's going to happen," I said, "is that Jago is going to sneak back here, tell Hamilton what's happened, and Hamilton is going to dash in here all wild-eyed and say Cuba's horse has come back without her and that he's afraid something has happened. He's got to go in search of the dear girl."

"Then what?"

"Then," I said, "I'll know that my theory is correct but what the rest of my theory is I would rather not tell you at this time because you would realize what a completely heartless, fiendish bastard we are dealing with and you would panic on me. I'm putting that moment off as long as I can."

For a second she just glared at me, and despite our predicament, despite the wind rising outside, despite it getting darker and the house getting spookier, I was enjoying myself. And Laura sensed it.

"Hah! You hope I *will* panic, don't you?"

I couldn't resist it. "Hope *you* panic? After last night? No, thank you, ma'am." I didn't want her thinking I had forgotten that little episode and what it entailed. She kept on acting like it was all over and settled, and got back to the matter at hand.

"I still think the whole thing is ridiculous," she said, and with that she huffed out. I thought at first she was going to her room but instead she went across the hall into the other parlor and started looking out the window. I knew what that meant.

Sure enough, a few minutes later she came back in and sat down—by me. She looked a whole lot paler than when she had left and I knew what that meant, too.

"Did you see him?" I asked real casually.

"See who?" she snapped.

"Jago," I said. "You were looking for him out of that window, weren't you? You see him sneaking back?"

She sighed and nodded. "I *think* I saw him. There was something out there in the trees. It might have been a deer or a ..."

She stopped. Mattie was calling up the backstairs to Hamilton. We couldn't make out what she was saying but the tone of her voice told me what she wasn't saying.

"She's not telling him about any deer," I said. "Get set."

About a minute later we heard Hamilton coming down the stairs. He came into the parlor putting on his rain gear and trying to look grieved instead of panicky.

"Farrell, are you sure you didn't see any trace of Cuba?"

Laura and I both got to our feet.

"Sure, I'm sure," I said, getting belligerent. "Why? What's happened?"

His eyes narrowed and then he decided for the second time that I didn't know anything. He looked from me to Laura.

"It's nothing, dear. Mattie just saw Cuba's horse come in without her. She's probably had a fall. Jago and I are going out to look for her."

He was making like a gentleman again. I fixed that.

"But Jago's sick."

"He's feeling much better."

I kept pressing him.

"I'll go with you."

"No, goddammit," he snarled, "we'd wind up hunting for you, too."

With that final display of graciousness, he was off. A minute or so later we heard the jeep tear down the driveway. I watched from the window. When I turned around, Laura was glaring at me.

"All right, Sherlock, you called your shot. Let's have the rest of it."

"You mean you still don't get it?" I asked. "It's so simple. They were keeping Cuba on ice. She was supposed to die later from a stray bullet ... a stray bullet from a deer rifle."

Laura blinked.

"But I still don't see … Look. Mary Belle is dead and if Cuba was found dead from a bullet from *his* rifle … well, that would make *two* murders …"

"Just a second," I said. "Think back now. Did Hamilton shoot that rifle even once this morning?"

She thought back and the blood started draining from her face. Then she was shaking her head and the "No" was just a rasp.

"You see, now?" I asked, not gloating any more. "The stray bullet that was supposed to kill Cuba was going to be from a deer rifle that only *you* had shot. Gentleman John Hamilton was going to make *you* the murderer!"

CHAPTER EIGHT

was lucky. Most girls, upon discovering that some ardent admirer has been playing them for a pigeon instead of a lovebird, tend to become a little morose. Not Laura. She just got indignant.

"Pete Farrell," she said, flouncing to her feet so she could look more outraged, "he wouldn't dare do that to me."

I sighed and got to my feet too. "You mean he is a poor enough sport to have Cuba knocked off but too good a sport to blame it on you."

She glared at me, still acting like a little girl who had suddenly been told there wasn't any Santa Claus.

"I still don't believe it. Men are horrible but they aren't *this* horrible."

I took her arm.

"Women just seem to have the knack for inspiring us to new depths. Come on upstairs. You need a big jolt of Old Faith Restorer?'

She babbled all the way up the stairs trying to knock holes in my story. I ushered her into my room, sat her down and poured her a drink that would have made an alcoholic shudder. She choked it down and the shock of it shook her loose from her last illusion about Gentleman John Hamilton.

"All right," she wheezed, "he's a dirty, dirty, *dirty* old man and everything you've said about him is …"

She stopped. Miss Maude had come out of her room down the hall. I sat down on the bed and we waited until we heard her heading downstairs. Then Laura leaned forward in her chair and whispered real ominously, "I wonder how much *she* knows."

"Nothing," I said. "Or else she and Hamilton are the greatest brother-sister act since the Barrymores."

"But what made Hamilton so sure that Cuba had the journal? How would he *know* that Miss Maude hadn't really just misplaced it. Maybe Miss Maude told him in secret that nobody but Cuba could have taken it and all this fussing he's been doing at her is just a cover-up."

"Look," I sighed, "if I thought that nice, old lady was a murderer, too, I'd put you on my back and swim out of here right now. That would be just too damn much. Three murderers, okay, but not *four*."

"Then, how could Hamilton have been so sure about Cuba?"

"He probably wasn't sure she had the journal," I said, "but if she tried sneaking off the island it would prove that she did and there was just one way for her to sneak off and that was on the boat. So he had Jago fake being sick and sneak down to the boat and wait for her. When she showed up, they went into their hunting-accident routine ... which they probably mapped out last night."

Laura shook her head like she still found it hard to believe. "But it sounds so complicated. I don't see why they ever thought they could get away with it."

"Complicated?" I said. "All they had to do was get the rifle away from you and then wait for me to come in. *I* was the only thing they hadn't counted on. They didn't figure that Miss Maude would talk me and my hangover clean out of the house. But when I came back in acting all innocent they were all set.

"Jago sneaked back down to the boat all set to take Cuba out to some spot that he and Hamilton had probably already decided on, some spot that would be in the general area of all that wild shooting you were doing."

Laura swallowed hard. "Then he was going to shoot her? Just like that?"

I nodded.

"Just like that. *With* the rifle you had used. With the wind and the rain and all that big-mouthing Hamilton was doing at lunch we never would have heard the shot. Then tomorrow they were going to find the body and call the coroner in.

"He would call it another one of those unfortunate deer-hunting accidents. And you would be it. You were the only one doing any shooting and the ballistic boys would prove that the bullet was from your rifle."

"But what about the big bump that you said Jago raised on Cuba's head?"

"That wouldn't have helped you," I said. "Nobody could prove that she hadn't gotten it when you *shot* her off the horse. You couldn't prove that the horse hadn't dragged her a little piece with her foot hung in the stirrup and she'd hit her head on a rock or a log enroute."

She kept fighting it.

"But if Jago had taken her to that spot there wouldn't be any horse tracks around."

"You're forgetting," I said, "that he still had her horse tied in the woods near the boat. He would have put her, unconscious the way she was, across the saddle and led the horse to the spot. And with all this rain you wouldn't be able to tell anything for sure about the tracks anyway.

"So they would have had you cold. Hamilton would have had you as an alibi to his whereabouts and Jago would have had Mattie to back up his lie about being sick in bed."

I got to my feet. "Now," I said, "are you ready to apologize? If I hadn't been a sex maniac as you say, if I hadn't followed Cuba, she'd be crying in her coffin thinking you had put her there."

I said it more to relax the tension than anything else but it just added to it ... to mine, not hers. She looked up at me, her eyes started flashing and she just spit out: "Damn him, I'll get him!"

It was the old Farrell luck again. Instead of having a scared girl on my hands, one I could control, all of a sudden I had a female Dick Tracy. *She's* gonna get a maniac and his two-hundred-and-sixty-pound hatchet man, she is.

"The hell you are!" I said. "You're not getting anybody. I'm getting 'em. All you're doing is what I tell you to do."

She sawed off that limb before I even realized I was out on it.

"Okay," she said, her eyes glittering, "go get 'em, Chief. Give me some orders."

I couldn't think of any so I sat back down on the bed, lighted a cigarette and acted like I wasn't aware that she was leering at me.

"All we can do," I said casually, "is wait for Hamilton to make his move."

"What kind of move?"

"Well, chances are," I said, "that Hamilton is going to go down to the boat and do a lot of screaming about Jago not tying Cuba up tight enough or hitting her hard enough and then they'll start searching."

"Searching? But if they think Cuba got loose herself, won't they wonder why she just didn't take off in the boat?"

I got to my feet again. "They'll probably figure that she found out she couldn't run the boat. Then they'll see the dinghy raising, probably find it washed up on the shore, figure she's still on the island and start trying to find her so they can finish her off."

"And when they don't find her?"

"Maybe Hamilton will crack under the strain," I said. "Maybe he'll get drunk and blab something about Mary Belle. Who knows? All we can do is wait."

"Sure," she said sarcastically. "Of course, we might try finding that journal, hunh? Don't you think Cuba might have just hidden it around this morgue some place? She didn't have saddle-bags and as tight as those riding pants and that sweater fit her, she couldn't have ridden off with anything that she couldn't hide in her mouth."

I can't stand smart-aleck girls, especially when they seem to be dead right.

"Well, don't think I haven't thought of that," I lied. "But have you thought of this? If Cuba could hide that thing where Hamilton, Jago, Mattie and Miss Maude couldn't find it, what chance have we got?"

She hadn't thought of that and I hadn't either until just then but it made sense. "So," I said, "the best thing for us to do is go down, have a little party with Miss Maude, get her drunk and try to pump her about what really happened that day before the hurricane."

She looked like her ears had gone bad on her. "Get *her* drunk? Farrell, don't you ever learn?"

"*I'm* not going to drink with her," I said. "*You're* going to drink with her and that's an order."

"Chicken!" she sneered. "Get your bottles."

Miss Maude had anticipated me slightly. When Laura and I walked into the parlor with my two bottles of Old Blabbermouth, she had already gone into action. She had ice, mixes and all sorts of deadly potions already lined up on the marble-topped table alongside the settee. But she appreciated our thinking of her.

"Oh, you sweet things!" she gurgled. "You came to cheer me up, didn't you? And I was going to cheer you two up. But you mustn't worry about Cuba. I'm sure it was just a little tumble and I'm sure she wouldn't want us to worry, would she? So we'll just have a little party and drink to her safe return. Peter, dear, what will you have?"

"Just mercy," I said, moving over to the table. "I'll tend bar. What'll you and Laura have?"

She got a big laugh out of that. "I just love him,' she told Laura. "Really, he's the ugliest-tempered guest we've ever had. When he snaps back at John I could just kiss him."

I couldn't help glowing a little at that and cut my eyes at Laura to show her that at least somebody appreciated me.

"Well, you kiss him for both of us, Miss Maude," she said. "I think he's terrible."

I decided to double the size of the drink I had started measuring out for her. Miss Maude laughed and said:

"I'm awfully disappointed in you two. I thought certainly with two such lovely people we'd have a romance. Peter, Laura is much more your type than Cuba."

I smiled and looked at Laura. "Just give me time, Miss Maude."

"Hah!" Laura said.

After an hour of my bar-tending she had mellowed considerably. She was sitting on the floor acting like an alcoholic Goldilocks, oohing and aahing at a bunch of old family photographs and daguerreotypes that Miss Maude had gotten out for us to look at.

As for Miss Maude she was still drinking like she had two livers, but I had been stoking her so heavy that her tongue was getting where it didn't fit her mouth. I was half sick from all the mix I had been drinking but things were going pretty well. I had Miss Maude talking about her journal and what a tragedy it was that we couldn't find it.

"Oh, Peter, we just must find it," she said. "I had this perfectly haunting passage about a mother sea turtle laying her eggs on the beach. Have you ever seen a mother turtle in labor? Simply fascinating. Like some huge gum machine—you know the kind with the round balls—giving birth."

I could just see her out there on the beach at night watching that damn turtle—probably patted it to console it—but that wasn't exactly the type of information I was after about the journal. Finally, though, after she had told me about some other haunting passages like that, we got down to the white meat—the last hurricane they'd had on the island.

"I'll bet that gave you plenty to write about," I said.

"Peter," she said expansively, "the very next hurricane we have I'm inviting you down. My own personal guest. You deserve a hurricane."

"He sure does," Laura said, not bothering to look up from her pictures. "Make it a big one."

Miss Maude laughed.

"Now, I don't mean it that way at all, Laura," she said. "I mean Peter, way down deep, has the soul of a true artist. He could appreciate a hurricane."

She followed that up with about two minutes of how a hurricane could be nature at its grandest: birth of the winds, the hand of God in your hair, etc., etc. I acted real impressed, slugged her with another drink and said:

"But, Miss Maude, as nice as hurricanes are, they can have their tragic side, too, can't they?"

She rolled her eyes at me and said, "You mean poor Mary Belle, don't you?"

I nodded. "But that happened before the hurricane really hit, didn't it?"

"The day before," she said. "That poor child … I'll never forget that morning." She shook her head at the thought of it. "I was standing at my window and saw her ride off between Jago and John. Poor dear, she had no idea what the day had in store for her."

Well, when she said that, naturally, I nearly fell off the settee. There it was: the *proof*. She hadn't seen Mary Belle off at the dock like she had told the police. She had been standing at her bedroom window and seen her drive off with Hamilton and Jago.

I had the case right in my hands. I tried to be casual about it. If I could get her to repeat that statement just one more time and get my tipsy little Goldilocks, Laura, to hear it, we had Hamilton … or at least a good hold on him.

"Miss Maude," I said, trying to keep my voice casual but at the same time trying to alert Laura with it, "did you say that the last time you saw Mary Belle was when you were standing at your …?"

I never finished. Laura let out this little shriek and started waving an old daguerreotype around.

"Miss Maude! This girl! This is the girl I saw last night. It wasn't Mary Belle's ghost, it was this girl's!"

CHAPTER NINE

I felt like a ball player about to slide home with the winning run when all of a sudden one of his teammates jumps off the bench and slugs him with a bat. That's what Laura had done to me. Miss Maude, all set to go on record as saying she hadn't seen Mary Belle off at the dock, but she never gets the chance because Laura starts blabbering that it wasn't Mary Belle's ghost she saw, it was that of the girl in the daguerreotype.

At first, I started to just reach out and calmly strangle her but then I realized that it was partly my fault, too, that she had started blabbering. After all, I had given her orders to drink with Miss Maude and anybody who could even mumble, much less blabber, after getting a nose in the same pan with her was doing all right.

So, I just gave her a hard look, shook my head at her and said, "Laura, I'm sure Miss Maude's not interested in any more of your ghosts. She was telling me about Mary Belle and how she saw her leave from ..."

She interrupted me again. "What are you shaking your silly head about? She is so interested." With that she raised up and kneeled in front of Miss Maude. "Look. Isn't that the girl?"

I made a grab for the daguerreotype but Miss Maude held on to it.

"Peter, she's right. This *is* the ghost." She beamed and passed the thing over to me. "It's great-aunt Elizabeth when she was a girl."

I took a look. The girl in the picture was twenty, maybe; blonde, had on a funny little hat, a bunch of these corkscrew type curls dangling down both sides of her head and even though she was pretty she looked like just the type who would enjoy flushing a boy out of bed with a girl at midnight. Real prim.

"You got *this* girl confused with Mary Belle?" I wheezed.

"Oh, I wish you had seen Mary Belle," Miss Maude said. "The resemblance is amazing. And Aunt Elizabeth has changed her hairdo. Don't you think she is wearing it page-boy now, Laura?"

I groaned but Laura ignored me. "I'm not certain, Miss Maude. I saw her just from the front but I remember that she was wearing it shoulder length so maybe …"

"No hat?" I asked.

"Whoever heard of a ghost wearing a hat?" she snapped, and then realized that I was just baiting her. "You still don't believe I saw her but …"

"All right," I sighed, "you saw her but let's talk about what Miss Maude saw." I was trying to tell her with my eyes to shut up and listen. "Now, Miss Maude, you were saying that the last you saw of Mary Belle was when she …"

She wasn't listening. "I wonder why Aunt Elizabeth is walking," she said, taking a final look at the picture and handing it back to Laura. "You know that no ghost ever walks without reason.

"Uncle Cyrus Hamilton walked because we put these northern friends of John's in his old room. Oh, he couldn't abide Yankees and he was just walking all over the place but then they left and we haven't seen him since."

"Miss Maude," I said, "that's real interesting but when Mary Belle …"

Laura again. "Miss Maude, why couldn't she be walking for the reason you said? She doesn't like the things that John

Hamilton has been writing about the family so she is going to walk the night and haunt this house until he stops it."

"Then why doesn't she haunt him?" I snarled. "Miss Maude, where did you say you were when Mary Belle drove off that last day with Jago and your brother?"

She gave me a restraining pat on the hand like I was a child interrupting his elders.

"Laura, I think you're exactly right, dear. Of course, I never saw Aunt Elizabeth walking until after Mary Belle drowned but then maybe she had been haunting John all along and he was too much of a spoil-sport to say anything about it."

"Miss Maude," I pleaded, "will you please forget Aunt Elizabeth and ..."

"So, now," Laura said, "Aunt Elizabeth is trying to get us to do something about him and ..."

That's the way it went the rest of that dark, dreary, maddening afternoon. I'd spend fifteen minutes getting Miss Maude off the subject of ghosts and back on her journal and the day of the hurricane but then either she or Laura would have some new thought on the spirit world and they would go galloping off after Aunt Elizabeth again.

I kept shaking my head at Laura as a signal that she could stop drinking but she would just stick her tongue out at me and have another blast. The only consolation I had was the thought of Hamilton out in that storm hunting for a girl who wasn't there. Then around five o'clock I heard the jeep drive up and go around the house. I jumped to my feet.

"Okay, girls," I said, "everybody up to their rooms."

For one thing, I didn't want Hamilton seeing them drunk and for another I wasn't sure what Laura, in her state, might say to him. She hadn't seen him since finding out that he had tried to frame her with Cuba's murder. She and Miss Maude both stared at me and finally got me in focus.

"*You* go to your room," Laura said. "You're an old party-pooper."

"And we had so much fun yesterday, Peter," Miss Maude sighed.

They were both so looped that their jawbones were working east and west instead of north and south so I did the only merciful thing. I put Miss Maude over one shoulder, Laura over the other and headed for the stairs.

"We're all going to go up and have a nice cold shower."

They started laughing and enjoying the ride. Hamilton didn't think it was so funny. Just as I got half-way up the stairs, he came in the back way and started that old goddammit routine of his.

"Goddammit, Farrell," he bellowed, "what are you doing with that girl?" He meant Laura and then he got a better look and saw that I had Miss Maude over my other shoulder. "*Goddammit,* man, that's my sister you've …"

Miss Maude drowned him out. "We're all going to take a shower."

He really started bellowing for me to put them down, then. I figured I'd just better keep going.

"You find Cuba?" I hollered over my shoulder.

"No! We came back for lights. Now, dammit, do as I …"

"What about a search party from the mainland?" I interrupted.

"We're cut off from the mainland. Now, dammit, put them down and if you ever get another woman drunk in this house, I'm …"

That was too much. I turned around on the stairs and faced him.

"What the hell are you complaining about?" I said. "I was the one who had to spend the afternoon with them."

Laura and Miss Maude must have looked even more ridiculous front view than back.

"Farrell! Put them down!"

"You take your sister," I said. "I'll take Laura."

I went on up and put Miss Maude down at the head of the stairs. She waved good-bye to Laura, Laura waved back to her and I kept going down the hall to Laura's room. Once inside, I dumped her on the bed, took off her shoes and went in and turned on the cold water in the tub. I was afraid that, in her shape, she couldn't keep her feet in a shower.

Then, I went back in all set to give her hell. I never got around to it. She had taken her dress off and was sitting on the side of the bed in her slip. It was like she had taken the top off of a three-pound box of candy.

"Farrell," she leered, "you know why you'll never make a good detective? You can't drink, that's why. I'm going to give you a shower."

With that she started to take her slip off, too, and for the next thirty seconds I thought I was going crazy. There I was, poor, tortured, sex-starved Pete Farrell, wrestling a beautiful, laughing, squirming girl around a room trying to keep her from taking all her clothes off. When a man gets that much out of character he can't help but think he's losing his mind.

Finally, I got the bedspread around her, wrapped her up in it like a mummy, flopped her on the bed and kept her there, still laughing, squirming and taunting me until the tub got full enough. Then, I asked her if she would get in it by herself or would I have to put her in it. She tried sitting up. "I'm going to put you in it."

I picked her up like she was a rug, and carried her kicking and squealing into the bathroom. Then I held her over the tub, held on to the end of the spread and let it unroll. There was the damnedest splash and gasp I ever heard come from a tub. While she spluttered, I got her out a towel and told her to call me when she got dressed.

I closed the door, went into my room, broke out a new bottle and had a big drink myself. With nothing but that ginger ale in me my stomach was beginning to think I had lost my mind too. Then I lay down on the bed to wait for her to call me but I hadn't figured on how worn out you get herding drunks. The next thing I knew, it was about three hours later and Laura was knocking at the door.

I sat up, looked at my watch and mumbled for her to come in. She was dry, dressed and, while the nap she had taken hadn't sobered her up it had left her just dormantly tight.

"How was I?" she asked, looking real guilty.

"Just great," I said. I got to my feet and told her to come in before she fell in. She sighed, put her hand to her head, came in, eased into a chair and looked at me suspiciously.

"Aren't you just being nice? Don't I remember you looking like you could kill me?"

She had changed into a little, soft, pink, short-sleeved sweater and a navy blue skirt and looked almost as nice as she had in that slip. I smiled and told her that she knew I'd never want to kill her.

"Of course, for a couple of hours I wanted to strangle you or tear out your tongue, but kill you, no."

She sighed again. "We talked about ghosts, didn't we? The picture of that girl? Aunt Elizabeth?"

"It wasn't what you said," I explained, "it was when you said it. You started talking about Aunt Elizabeth just as Miss Maude started talking about not seeing Mary Belle off at the dock."

She stared at me.

"Miss Maude admitted that she didn't see her when she left?"

I nodded. "But I don't think she realized she said it any more than you did." I filled her in on what had happened and she started looking even sicker.

"I'm sorry."

I walked over, gave her a fatherly little pat on the head and told her to forget it.

"At least we know the truth now. She's lying for Hamilton and tonight we'll get the whole story. We'll keep *her* drinking. We default."

"Thanks," she groaned and then looked up at me curiously. "Don't I remember seeing that s.o.b. Hamilton?"

I told her she did. "He said he still hasn't found Cuba but I think he's found the dinghy or he would have looked a lot more desperate than he did."

"Desperate?" she said. "All I remember him looking is upside down."

"You were over my shoulder. You and Miss Maude."

"Miss Maude, too?"

"You drank her to a draw," I said, and went over and poured her out a big drink. "Take this. It'll either settle your stomach or rearrange it so you can live with it."

She gulped it down, harnessed it on the third bounce and put it to work for her. Then, with her eyes still watering and a funny smile on her face, she looked up at me.

"Don't I remember something else? The tub? Me in my slip?"

"Yeah," I said. "I tried to get you to take it off but for some reason you wouldn't listen to me."

Her smile got bigger and her memory got better.

"You're lying. I was going to take everything off and give you a shower but you wouldn't let me. You wrapped me up in that bedspread." She started blushing and then said softly, "Thank you, Pete."

I fought back a shudder. The situation was about to go from plain horrible to downright grisly. I was falling in love with the girl. That drink she had just taken had done it. She wasn't only the cutest, prettiest girl I'd ever met, she was the gamest. But the thing was, I didn't want to fall in love with her. I changed the subject.

"We'd better go down to Miss Maude," I wheezed. "I'll get cleaned up."

It didn't work. She kept gazing up at me and her smile started fading. She could see in my eyes that I was falling in love with her. But what she couldn't see was what it was all going to lead up to at bedtime.

Downstairs things were better. Just as I had hoped, Hamilton had grabbed a bite to eat and then dashed out into the night with Jago to hunt for Cuba some more. And as I had also hoped, Miss Maude had tottered back down, opened up another bottle and thrown away the cork. The world's gamest women, that's who I was surrounded by.

"Peers, Cheeter!" she said.

The two and a half hours after dinner I will always remember as the most unsporting of my life. I hate the idea of ganging up on anybody and that's what we were doing to Miss Maude. Laura had drunk with her all afternoon and here I was taking over after dinner. She made a good fight of it but with that two gallons of warm ginger ale in me for a base, she didn't have a chance. By ten o'clock the poor old thing was turning her soul wrong side out.

It started when the talk turned to Cuba. She tried to act like she had accepted Hamilton's story that Cuba had probably just broken a leg in a tumble from the horse and they would find her before the night was over and everything would be all right. But then she broke down and got maudlin.

She said she had the feeling that Cuba had been killed in the fall from the horse but no matter how she had died the people in Queensport would blame John for it. When she said that, her lips started trembling, her chin wrinkled up and I though she was going to cry.

"They even think he had something to do with Mary Belle's death," she said.

I felt so damn ashamed of myself for putting a slow mickey to such a nice old lady that I couldn't pull the trigger. Laura, though, remembering that the object of the nice old lady's pity had tried to hang a murder around her neck, came through.

"Miss Maude, you don't mean it?" she said, acting astonished. "John Hamilton murdering somebody? Why that's the most ridiculous thing I ever heard."

That did it. Miss Maude said that it *was* ridiculous and that's why she had lied to Tom Gill, the County Chief of Police, about having seen Mary Belle off at the dock the day she drowned.

"John felt just terrible about having to ask me to do it but I told him he was being silly. We both knew that they would believe me where they would suspect him no matter what he and Jago said. And it's so unfair. He's never done a thing to those people except refuse to let them use our beaches and hunt and fish on the island."

That took care of Hamilton's alibi! And I would have felt even guiltier about the way it had been done, if Miss Maude hadn't added:

"And, of course, John knew that they would try to make something of the fact that poor Jago had already murdered one person."

Laura gave a gasp and she wasn't acting. "Jago? A murderer?"

"Not really, dear," Miss Maude smiled sadly. "It was purely self-defense but the poor thing still had to serve eight years. John was the only one who would give him work when he got out."

All I could think of was Ben Ponza. That bastard hadn't sent Laura and me down after just a couple of suspected murderers; he knew that one of them was a *confirmed* murderer. Jago couldn't have killed a man in self-defense. Who in hell would ever pick on a monster like him!

"Miss Maude," I sighed, "what about us all turning in now?"

She was so drunk and so close to a crying jag that she didn't protest. I took her by one arm, Laura took her by the other and we headed for the stairs with her still confessing. She said that she knew that John had his faults but underneath he was kind and gentle. It was just that he had been hurt.

He was really the most distinguished member of the whole Hamilton line, considering his accomplishments, but the people in Queensport and throughout the state still regarded old Joshua Hamilton and John's father as *the* Hamiltons.

All the way upstairs she kept that up. She thought the refusal of his own people to recognize his worth was the main reason he had never left the island. He wanted to become so famous with his writing that they would be forced to recognize Spanish Point as John Hamilton's island.

She said that was the reason she had never married. John needed someone who understood him. She carried on along that line and by the time we got her to her room I was about to go on a crying jag myself. And she sensed it. She made a good try at smiling and apologized for getting maudlin. Then she tried to get funny. She patted Laura's hand and said:

"Now, dear, you get a good night's sleep and don't worry about Cuba or Aunt Elizabeth either. Cuba's really all right, probably, and if Aunt Elizabeth walks tonight I'll tell her not to dare go near your room."

That finished Laura off. All through Miss Maude's recital of her sorrows, she had been getting soberer and sadder. The mention of Aunt Elizabeth brought back all the horror of the night before. With the storm howling outside worse than ever, she looked, for a second, like she wanted to crawl in Miss Maude's bed and pull the covers over her head. How much simpler it would have been if she had.

Instead, she squared her shoulders, forced a smile, joined me in telling Miss Maude good night, and then accompanied me back down the hall to her room. I opened the door for her. She stared into that big dark room, turned, looked up at me, flashed that brave, little smile again and said:

"Well, we did it. If we could only find Mary Belle's body, now, I think we would have him."

I ignored that. It wasn't what she was thinking at all. I could see it in her eyes. She was thinking about the low, miserable, fiendish thing she was going to do to me. I hardened my heart, told her good night just as casually as I could and went into my room and started giving myself hell.

"Farrell," I said, "you're not in love with this girl. After what she's done to you, you couldn't be. Now, don't be a damn fool."

I changed into my pajamas, brushed my teeth, shaved, showered and got into bed. When I heard Laura come into the bathroom and start messing around, I said my prayers:

"Lord, please give me the presence of mind to remember that this girl took advantage of me. Then, please, give me the strength to take advantage of her. Amen."

Then, I got a magazine off the night table, propped myself up in bed, and started reading and waiting. After Laura left the bathroom, I knew it wouldn't be long. The wind was howling and banging shutters and blowing limbs and stuff across the porch. Then, it came … a knock on the bathroom door.

I steeled myself. "Farrell," I said, "this is it. Think, now. Think of who got you into this murderous mess. Think of all the indignities you have suffered at the hands of women in the last forty-eight hours. Don't think of anything else. Just that."

"Laura?" I called out.

The door slowly opened and she came in. She had on a pale blue negligee and a little white, low-necked nightgown with a ringlet of pink bows around the top. She was the loveliest thing I ever saw. Also the scaredest.

"Pete," she said, fighting to keep from whimpering, "we made a bargain. You kept your part of it. Now, I'm going to keep mine."

CHAPTER TEN

"Courage, Farrell!" this voice inside me said. "Don't even look at her. You don't really love her. Besides, she's probably an old hand at this business. She may look all sweet and lovely and pure and innocent but she works in New York, remember?"

I didn't say a word to her. I sat up, took one of the pillows out from behind my head, put it on what would be her side of the bed and pulled back the cover. In that second, I knew I had been right about her fiendish little scheme. She was thinking I'd feel so sorry for her that I would just protect her and wouldn't make her go through with the bargain.

She stared at the bed, stared at me, swallowed hard and started back to her room. Then some place a shutter banged in the wind. It must have sounded like a lid banging shut on a coffin. She cringed, gave me this brave, little smile, turned back to the bed and started slowly taking off the pale blue negligee.

It was like a beautiful butterfly coming out of a cocoon. I tried to act unconcerned and went back to my magazine again like I was reading but I held it so that I could watch her out of the corner of my eye. That was what caused all the trouble.

First, I saw how nervous she was. It was like she really never had been in bed with a man before. That made me feel even sorrier for her. But then, when she was in nothing but that little white nightgown, she leaned forward to get in bed and the top of the gown sort of billowed out at the top and revealed a vista of such loveliness that I lost control of the situation.

Up to then, despite all the hard talking I had been doing to myself, I knew subconsciously that I wasn't going to make her go through with the bargain. But when I saw what I did, it just set me on fire and my conscience went up in flames. It was like Adam taking his first bite of the apple. In that moment he saw Eve and all the glories of the flesh and he was helpless. It was too late to spit the apple out. The evil was in his blood. And that's the way it was with me.

But I still watched her just out of the corner of my eye. She kept her right foot on the floor while she put her left leg in bed. The feel of the sheet made her start to draw it back but that shutter banged again. Then she was all the way in bed and the mattress began to feel like a big battery ... electric currents were shooting all through it.

Then she gave this big sigh and settled back on the pillow. It was like some human sacrifice settling down on an altar. I nearly tore the corners out of both my eyes watching her. Her eyes were closed, her lips were parted and one of the straps had slipped down off her shoulder.

I kept trying to act like I was reading. But then all the letters started looking like phallic symbols. Well, I couldn't stand it any longer. Very slowly I reached over and put the magazine on the night table. And just as slowly I turned back on my side facing Laura and slid down between the sheets.

A shiver seemed to run through her and her lips parted even more. They were the warmest looking, the most inviting lips I'd ever been close to, much less in bed with. I raised up a little on my right elbow and my left hand crept across the sheet to her upper arm and came to rest between it and the sheet.

I was trembling even more than she was. Then I brought my right hand up and it crept across the sheet, too, and then it was creeping across her breasts to her far shoulder. It wasn't just trembling, it was shaking like it had some sort of amatory palsy.

Then I was half over her and my right hand wasn't shaking any more. It was like it had severed connections with the rest of my body and was operating as an independent unit. It started creeping towards the shoulder strap of hers that had slipped down.

She started breathing faster and her lips parted even more. Then the hand closed around the strap and started retreating down her upper arm. The upper part of the nightgown started retreating with it and the farther it retreated the more breathtaking everything became. Then I blacked out.

The next thing I knew I was kissing her, forcing her lips ever further apart. The hand that had held the gown was at her bare breast. The other hand had the frilly hem of her gown sliding it upwards along her leg, then along her thigh.

Then I felt the tears on my cheek. The hottest tears God ever let issue from the eyes of woman. Then they weren't tears. They were smears of acid eating into my dirty, rotten soul.

I blacked out again. When I came to this time, I was on my feet stomping around in the middle of the room snarling, "Goddammit! Goddammit! Goddammit!"

I don't usually curse that bad in front of girls but I must have said that word fifteen times. I wanted to be a lecher, I wanted to take advantage of her but I just couldn't make myself do it. Women ought to have their tear ducts removed at birth.

Finally, when the seizure was over, I glared at Laura. She was just lying there with the covers pulled up under her chin and her eyes closed. I started getting mad all over again.

"Come on!" I said. "We'll push those beds together in your room and you can hold my goddam hand."

She shook her head. She didn't want any part of the "ghost" room. Which made me even madder.

"Look," I said, "I'm not one of these movie hero nuts. I'm not going to sit up in a chair all night and watch you sleep. Is that what you want?"

She shook her head again.

"Well, what *do* you want," I asked her. "You want to sleep with me?"

She nodded.

"But brother and sister?" I said.

She nodded again.

"You still don't think I'll take advantage of you? All night in one bed and you don't think I'll go berserk and …?"

She shook her head.

"Dammit, stop shaking your head," I said. "Say something."

She opened one eye. "I'm scared."

I sighed and went over to the bed and stared down at her.

"Would you mind telling me just one thing? Have you ever been to bed with a man before?"

She shook her head. "No. I'm sorry."

I started saying "goddammit" again. The only twenty-four-year-old virgin in New York City and I had to get her in a situation like we were in. I glared at her even harder and she closed the one eye. I went over and pulled the blanket back from the sheet. She opened both eyes and watched me.

"You," I said, "are going to sleep *under* the sheet. I'm going to sleep on top of it. And God help you if you get between them. I'm not going to be responsible any more."

With that I got in bed, under the blanket and on top of the sheet, snatched the magazine off the table and started acting like I was reading. The words started crawling around again, looking like snakes mating. But I kept staring at them and she knew that was all I was doing, just staring. She turned on her side, snuggled up and put her hand on my arm. It was like a blow torch snuggling up to a barrel of gunpowder.

"Thank you," she murmured.

"*Don't* touch me!" I snapped.

"You're the sweetest boy I ever met."

I told her curtly that if I was sweet, I never would have touched her in the first place.

"And take that hot hand off of me."

She moved the hand up across my chest and gave a big sigh.

"I'll make it up to you."

I put the magazine down and glared at her.

"You mean that?"

She nodded.

"You mean," I said slowly, "that at some future date you're going to bed with me and there's not going to be any sheet between us?"

She nodded again. I sat up and put the magazine aside.

"Look," I said. "You're not scared any more, are you, and you know I'm not going to make you go through with our bargain, don't you?"

She nodded and smiled.

"Well," I said, fighting to keep from whining, "if this thing is going to happen, can you think of a better time than now? After all, I kept you from taking your clothes off once and then when I had you with all your clothes and three fourths of a nightgown off, I stopped. Now, if it's going to happen, why can't it happen now?"

"Because we're not married yet."

I almost jumped out of bed.

"By God, you're worse than Cuba!" I said. "She tortured me but she never threatened to marry me."

My life's plans didn't call for me to get married until I was sixty and then not to any writer. Laura didn't seem to realize that, though.

"Cuba couldn't threaten you," she said. "She knew you weren't in love with her." She grinned and tried pulling me back down in bed with her. "But you're in love with me and if you don't marry me, I'll tell your mother that you slept with me."

And that would be all it would take, too. She would be just the type that my mother and the Old Man would love and after she told them about the bargain we made, they'd put a shotgun in my back and down the aisle we would go. I slumped back down in the bed and reached for her.

"Well, if I'm going to sleep with you, I'm really going to sleep with you."

She laughed and pushed me away.

"If you do, I'll go back to my room."

"And Aunt Elizabeth?"

"I won't think about her. I'll just think about you being in here feeling sorry for me in there and wishing you hadn't been such a stinker and that I was in here with you."

I sighed and turned her loose. She snuggled up to me again and talked for an hour I guess. She told me she was from a small town, too—in Maryland. She had gone to New York to be a career girl. The world's greatest writer. No time for marriage. At least, not until she had become editor of *Chic* magazine and, maybe, won a Nobel prize.

But I had looked so adorable banging around the room and saying "goddammit", that she knew she couldn't wait for all of that. We would be a husband-wife team. But since she was the writer, I would have to take orders from her.

Even in her sleep she managed to torture me. I dreamed that we were married and were on our honeymoon and there weren't any covers between us. Then I dreamed that I wasn't dreaming. That woke me up. There *weren't* any covers between us.

It was morning and somehow during the night she had wiggled out from under the sheet and under the blanket with me. How she had done it I didn't know but there she was asleep in my arms and nothing between us but one sheer, little nightgown and one pair of thin pajamas.

Now a man at midnight can be expected to have at least a spark of conscience but not a man who awakens all warm and drowsy on a cold, rainy morning with a beautiful girl all snuggled up in his arms.

Gently, I drew her to me. Softly, I kissed her. Slowly, she opened her eyes and slowly the fear and surprise in them receded. Lovingly, her arms went around my neck. And, maddeningly, the goddam door exploded into sound.

"Mr. Farrell! It's Jago! Get up. We found Miss Cuba. You got to come with us!"

CHAPTER ELEVEN

was getting to be the Ulysses of the sex world. Every time I would be just about to make it to port I'd get knocked off course. This time it was Jago banging on die door. He had a set of knuckles like a house detective. And he was using them as though he knew I had a beautiful girl in bed with me and was trying to knock us out of it with sound waves.

"Jago," I bellowed, keeping my hold on Laura, "if you hit that door one more time, I'm …"

Laura clapped her hand over my mouth and he clobbered the door again.

"Mr. Farrell, you hear me? Mr. John's down at the dock with Miss Cuba. He wants you and Miss Maude to come down in the station wagon. I'm going on back."

With that he was gone. And for a dumb brute he had put on a damn fine act. Laura started trying to get out of my arms.

"Damn you, Pete Farrell, you said you saved that girl's life and took her to Queensport."

"She *is* in Queensport," I said, pulling her back to me. "Now, just relax."

She managed to get up on one elbow and then gave me this amazed look.

"Relax? You aren't serious? Two murderers out there waiting to …"

"Waiting to kill me," I said, "and they probably will and you're going to hate yourself the rest of your life because you had the chance to make my last hours real pleasant and didn't. But I'm not going to let you do yourself that way."

The spell was broken but she proceeded to stomp on the pieces. She started laughing and fought her way up into a sitting position.

"No, I'm not going to let you do *yourself* this way. If I let you make love to me, you wouldn't have anything to live for and you'd get careless and would get killed."

She gave a big sigh, wiggled over on to her side of the bed, shook her head and leered at me.

"You almost had me, didn't you, Farrell? And I said not until we get married and I meant it." Then she got serious. "Now, what are they up to?"

I gave up. I slid out of bed and headed for my clothes on the back of the chair.

"They're bluffing," I said. "They've probably realized that she's not on the island and they think that I had something to do with getting her off of it. Turn your head."

She turned her head while I got into my shorts.

"But why would they say they've found her?" she asked. "And why do they want you to come down to the dock?"

"Some sort of trap," I said. "When they spring it, they figure I'll give myself away and they'll *know* what happened to Cuba."

"Then what?"

"Then they're going to kill me."

She turned back around and couldn't help laughing.

"Farrell, that death-bed routine isn't going to get you back in this bed. Besides, they wouldn't kill you in front of Miss Maude. And besides that, you were born to suffer. You'll live forever."

That was a helluva comforting thought. I finished dressing and got my rain gear out. By that time Laura was up and in her negligee. She kissed me good-bye and I felt sorry for Hamilton and Jago. If they tried anything that would keep me from laying siege to this warm, beautiful thing again they were as good as dead.

When I got downstairs, Miss Maude, looking like a hung-over toad, was fidgeting around the parlor waiting for me. She gave me a weary, bleary-eyed smile, handed over the keys to the station wagon and started telling me how exasperated she was with brother John.

"Evidently Cuba's all right or he wouldn't be playing such silly games," she fumed, "but he gave Jago strict orders not to tell us a word about what has happened. He wants us to come down to the dock and *he'll* tell us. Now can you make any sense out of that?"

"Miss Maude," I said, building for the future, "I'm just so glad they've found Cuba that I don't care whether it makes any sense or not."

I went out back to bring the station wagon around and a finer day for foul deeds I never saw. The rain had stopped for a spell but the sky wasn't more than tree-top high, and a gale that must have been doing fifty was herding these tufted grayish black clouds along like they were a bunch of dirty sheep. Then there would be a big gust that would frisk the oaks of all their rotten limbs and the air would all of a sudden look like a floating jack-straw game.

I drove around front for Miss Maude and she came out in galoshes and a big, hooded raincape that caught the wind like a kite. I grabbed her and got her into the car before she sailed off … not realizing just how handy that flapping cape would turn out to be.

We churned and splashed along the road through the woods and about twenty minutes later came out at the dock … only it looked more like the ferry landing to hell, things were so dismal.

The wind had shifted so that it was coming straight over the marshes out front of us, and with them being flooded, it looked like the whole world was just clouds, wind and water. And standing right on the brink of this world, all bearded and red-eyed, with their rain gear flapping in the wind, were my two little playmates.

I stopped about five feet from where they were standing and rolled down the window. Miss Maude saved me the trouble of having to think up a greeting. She leaned across me and yelled:

"John, what's all this nonsense about? Where's Cuba? Is she hurt?"

He ignored her and kept glaring at me.

"Get out of the car," he hollered above the wind. "Both of you."

With those words, he wrecked his whole production. Only I didn't know it until Miss Maude and I got out and I realized how much stronger the wind was out in the open.

It must have been doing seventy and with Miss Maude's cape flapping and mine and Jago's and Hamilton's rain gear flapping and Miss Maude being a little hard of hearing anyway, you had to almost scream to do any communicating.

Miss Maude started it off. "John," she screamed, "you stop this. Now, where's Cuba?"

He glared at me, leaned towards Miss Maude and cupped his hands to his mouth.

"Don't ask me, ask your Mr. Farrell."

I didn't bat an eye. Miss Maude did. With that hood of hers flapping in the wind she hadn't heard half of what he was saying.

"What did he say?" she yelled at me.

Right then I knew how to play it, how to turn Hamilton's little melodrama into low comedy. I blinked and turned to Jago.

"What did he say?"

"Goddammit," Hamilton shrieked, "you heard me. You followed Cuba here yesterday. You said you didn't."

I shook my head like I still couldn't understand him.

"I did *what?*"

He hollered something back but Miss Maude drowned him out demanding that we get in the car and talk. He grabbed her and started hollering into the hood of her rain cape.

"Farrell says he went just to the beach yesterday. He's lying. He followed Cuba here. Look!"

It was the pay-off. There in the mud near the planking of the dock was a brass button with a stag's head on it.

"That button came off that corduroy shirt he was wearing yesterday," he shouted. "He was *here*. Not at the beach like he said."

He was dead right about the button. It had come off of my shirt. And the ironic part about it was that it was probably the button that Cuba had been twisting that morning in the parlor when she was persuading me to go to the beach.

"What about the button?" I hollered at Hamilton.

He whirled from Miss Maude to me.

"You know damn well what. You followed Cuba here and raped her and hid her body some place. Now, where?"

It was the Moment of Truth, the moment in which I was supposed to become so outraged by the rape and murder charge that I would blurt out what I had really done with Cuba.

I didn't fall for it. But Hamilton got madder at Miss Maude than he did at me. She had caught just one word of his accusation.

"Rape?" she squawked. "Who's been raped?"

It was my turn to holler into the hood.

"Miss Maude, your brother claims that I followed Cuba here and raped her and murdered her and hid her body some place."

She came clean out from under the hood to get at Hamilton.

"You apologize for that, John Hamilton. Every time I turned around Cuba was trying to rape this poor boy. Now, you …"

He didn't let her finish. He grabbed her by the shoulders and started hollering in her good ear. Cuba hadn't been trying to rape me, he said; she was just taunting me. They had found hoofprints of Cuba's horse near the dock. I had followed her, probably tried to get her out on the boat and when she wouldn't go I had raped her and then killed her. Otherwise, why would I have pretended that I hadn't gone any place but the beach? He picked up the button.

"This *proves* he was here."

I took my turn at the good ear.

"Don't blame him, Miss Maude," I said. "The poor devil's just worn out. I wasn't down here at the dock at all yesterday. That button must be off the shirt I was wearing when we landed here the first day. I've got two shirts with buttons like that."

I did have and it just so happened that I *was* wearing the other one that first day. Hamilton and Jago both knew it and they also knew that I was using it to get out of the trap they had set for me. They hadn't forced me into admitting a thing. But they kept trying. Hamilton snarled that I was lying and then Jago got into the act.

All the time we had been talking he had been standing there glaring at me, trying to awe me with his size and acting like all he needed was just one word from Hamilton and he would reduce me to so much bone meal and bloody pulp.

"Mr. John," he hollered in Hamilton's ear, "we'll just *check* his buttons when we get back."

He was grinning, flashing all his bad teeth and looking like some sort of hairy gargoyle. A picture of him hitting Cuba flashed through my mind and I cut loose in Hamilton's other ear.

"If you check my buttons, you'd better check your insurance, first. I'll break you in half and beat that ape to death with your remains."

Jago wasn't sure what I had said and Miss Maude wasn't either.

"Not rape again?" she hollered.

"I didn't say 'rape,' " I hollered back. "I called him an ape."

That broke Hamilton's spirit. He gave up. He stepped between me and Jago, showed me the button and said he was keeping it until after the storm.

"Then we'll see what the police say."

With that he and Jago splashed over to the jeep, gave me one last loving look and roared off, headed back for the house. Miss Maude watched them go, put that flapping hood back over her head and I helped her into the station wagon.

"Peter," she said sadly, "you'll have to forgive him. The poor thing is just so upset about Cuba he doesn't know what he's doing."

"I understand perfectly, Miss Maude," I said, making my own private little joke, "but don't you go getting all upset, too. I've just got the feeling that everything is still going to turn out all right."

An hour or so later I had showered, changed into dry clothes, eaten a fast breakfast and was back in my room telling Laura what had happened. After I was through and she had finished laughing about Miss Maude and her flapping cape, she came up with a very good question. *Why* had it happened?

"He must have had more in mind than just trying to put the blame on you, Pete."

"I think he did have," I said. "And still has."

I had two theories: first, there was the business of testing my reactions to the charges of rape, murder, body snatching, etc. If

I squealed loud enough they would know that I hadn't helped Cuba escape and that she was still on the island and no doubt dead. If not from exposure, then from the lick on the head. That way they were home free. Cuba couldn't talk and they could blame the head injury on her fall from the horse.

"But," I said, "if they figured from my reaction that I had helped her escape to the mainland, then finding that button would give them a fighting chance."

And it still would, *if* Jago had slugged her from behind when she got on the boat. That way she wouldn't be able to positively identify her attacker. Hamilton and Jago could say that I had done it in the heat of passion, gotten scared and rushed her over to the mainland, making up a lie about Jago enroute.

"If that's the case," I said, "it'll just be my word against theirs and Jago has at least two people who'll swear that he was in his room all morning. And besides, all it would amount to at most would be a simple case of assault and battery."

Laura shook her head and then brightened. "But look, Pete. When Cuba regains consciousness over there, she can tell the police where the journal is, they can come over here, find it *and* the evidence about Mary Belle. Not assault and battery. Murder. So what are we worried about?"

"Just a couple of minor details," I said, "like how do we know for sure that they didn't intercept the journal or that they haven't found it. That's the only concrete evidence in the case. And that's supposing that the journal is at the bottom of all this."

"But," she said, "we can still tell the police that Miss Maude was lying when she alibied for Hamilton about seeing Mary Belle off at the dock."

"Yeah," I said, "and she can come right back and say that she was drunk and doesn't remember a thing about telling us that. If she lied once, she'll do it again."

Laura sighed and agreed. "And of course, there's the little matter of no corpse."

"Unless," I said, "there was some hint in the journal about what could have happened to the corpse. If …"

I stopped. Someone was coming down the hall. I motioned for Laura to keep quiet.

"It's Hamilton," she whispered.

It was. He walked on down past Miss Maude's room and then we heard a door open. Laura's eyes lit up and she got all breathless.

"Cuba's room. He's gone in there."

I nodded and started taking off my shoes. "I'm going, too."

"Are you crazy?" she asked, coming over and kneeling by me. "You know the way that hall creaks. He'll hear you sure."

"Not the route I'm taking."

I eased through the door that led out on the porch. With the storm howling even worse, there wouldn't be anybody outside to see me, and nobody inside could hear me. I took the same route that Cuba had taken coming to my room.

After about twenty seconds of creeping along, I was outside the French doors looking into her room. And there Hamilton was. He was searching the room and getting madder by the second.

Finally, he worked his way over to the bed. He turned the mattress back from the bottom and looked. Then from the top. Then his face lit up and he yanked off all the covers and then the mattress cover. Then he stuck his hand in a big slit in the mattress. All he pulled out was cotton wadding.

I sneaked back down to my room and Laura met me at the door. I gave her the news: Cuba had hidden the journal in her mattress first, but then, evidently, she had moved it.

"It's still in this house some place and Hamilton's getting wilder all the time."

CHAPTER TWELVE

My gloating about Hamilton not having found the journal lasted just long enough for Laura to get all excited, pull me inside the room and say: "Well, what do we do now?"

I sighed and strolled over and sat down on the bed. "What can we do? Nothing but wait."

She reacted just the way I figured she would: put her hands on her hips, marched over to me and looked at me like I was crazy.

"But, Pete, you know he's hunting for the journal. We've got to find it before they do. Now, come on."

"Look," I said, "if they find us snooping around, they'll know that we know what's going on. Right now they aren't sure of it and that's what's running Hamilton nuts."

"So we just sit here and wait?"

"Wait and hope that he doesn't find it and hope that the pressure of not finding it will make him show his hand some way." I stretched out on the bed. "Wake me when something happens. I had this strange pressure on my spine last night and didn't get much sleep."

"Pete Farrell," she snapped, "if you go to sleep, Hamilton won't shoot you, I will."

She saw to it that I didn't. She went into her room, came back with a manicure kit and sat down and started doing her nails. When she wasn't making my flesh crawl with her filing, these strange noises I kept hearing around the house were. After about an hour of it and no shouts of "Eureka" from Hamilton, I decided to try a little experiment.

"Laura," I said, raising up on an elbow, "if you've got any sporting blood at all I can get us some action."

Her eyes narrowed. "What kind?"

"I don't know," I said. "All I do know is that I can make somebody come in this room."

She blew on her nails. "How?"

"Just come over here, lie down on the bed with me and give me a long, passionate kiss."

She was so bored with just waiting around that she did just what I said. She bit her lip to keep from smiling, came over, got on the bed with me, gave me a long passionate kiss and, by damn, it happened.

Before I could even kiss her back, we heard what sounded like an army coming up the stairs. She drew away from me, waited, and here came the army down the hall. When whoever was leading it knocked on the door, she got to her feet and went back to her chair ... shaking her head and laughing to herself about the uncanny Farrell luck.

I got to my feet and growled, "Come in!"

In marched Miss Maude followed by Jago and Mattie. Mattie had a big tray with our lunch on it and Jago was loaded down with firewood. Their hearts weren't in their work but their spleens were. They both looked like they wanted to kill us.

Miss Maude was oblivious to it all. She said that with the mood poor John was in she thought that Laura and I would enjoy lunch more upstairs.

"And with that horrid storm out there I thought a fire would make things a little cheerier. Jago does make the cheeriest fires."

She must have seen the look Jago gave us because she stuck around until after he was gone. Then, despite our asking her to stay and have a drink with us, she said she had to go back down and commiserate with poor John.

"I've told him that I just don't believe that Cuba is on this island. They've searched it from one end to the other and I think it's just some thoughtless prank of Cuba's. I think that some way she has left the island." She sighed. "But telling John that doesn't cheer him up a bit. He's sending poor Jago out to search for her again."

With that she left and as soon as she did Laura headed for the bottle on the night table. She poured herself a drink so big it sounded like she was slopping hogs and I knew why. The hate in Jago's eyes had made her realize what a ticklish game we were playing. If Hamilton got *too* desperate, he could just give the word and Jago would try murdering us both. She gulped the drink down and turned to me. "Can't we do *something?*"

I felt the same way but I couldn't afford to let her know it "Yeah," I said, "let's eat." She looked down at the tray that Mattie had put on the big hassock between the two chairs in front of the fire.

"Not without a stomach pump handy. I'll bet every one of those sandwiches has got rat poison in the mayonnaise."

It was a damn good bet, considering the look in Mattie's eyes, but I told her she was being silly, and sat down and started eating. It helped to calm her down, all right. She poured herself an even bigger drink, curled up on the bed with it, and started telling me, in a tender sort of way, why she loved me so.

"You're so *manly,* Farrell. As long as you've got something to eat, drink or make love to, nothing else bothers you, does it?"

"Nothing," I lied, "except people knocking on doors or virgins with misspent lives trying to blackmail me into marrying them."

The last had just the effect I hoped it wculd. She smiled—archly—poured herself another drink, curled up again and started telling me how things were going to be when we did get married.

I acted like I didn't hear a word she was saying. That and the whiskey kept her talking. After I finished off the fruit cake, I got up, got my harp, sat back down and started playing soft and sweet. By then she was debating with herself about what to name our sixth child.

The next thing I knew she had dozed off. For once, too much whiskey, too fast, had done a nervous system some good. I just kept sitting there watching her, playing my harp and listening to the wind. Pretty soon I found myself dozing off, too. At first I fought it, thinking that when Laura got a little sounder asleep I'd go over and cuddle up with her. But then I fell asleep and what happened next still causes arguments in certain circles.

First, I had these crazy dreams about Laura and Cuba and then I was dreaming about that ghost, Aunt Elizabeth. I dreamed that she was right in the room with me, looking at me asleep in the chair by the fire. I could see her real plain. She was dressed in that same fancy green velvet dress that Cuba had worn the night she came to my room. And she was a whole lot prettier than she had been in that daguerreotype.

In fact, she was downright sexy. And she was happy, too. She gave me this big smile and then started strolling away towards the closet. I seemed to realize that here was a beautiful girl about to get away from me, and even though it was a dream I ran true to life. I made this lunge for her.

And that's when I woke up. But it wasn't any relief because I was looking straight across the room at the closet that Aunt Elizabeth had been heading for in the dream. The door had been closed before I went to sleep but now it was *open* … just enough for a girl the size of Aunt Elizabeth to get through.

I'll admit it, for a second my lungs felt like they had locked on me and my scalp started icing up. Then I realized how silly I was being. After all, I wasn't like Miss Maude or Laura, I was a sane, sensible, mature person who knew there wasn't anything to dreams, ghosts and all that supernatural jazz. The catch on the door was old and a draft from inside the closet had just blown the door open. Something simple like that. Besides, even if there were such things as ghosts, they wouldn't have to open doors, they'd go right on through 'em.

So, to prove to myself that my draft theory was right, I went over to the closet, went in, turned on the drop cord light, got down on my hands and knees and started feeling around the baseboards. Sure enough there was a draft. Due to the gradual sinking of the house's foundation, the baseboards had pulled away from the flooring by about an inch, and air rising from some inner recess of the house was flowing through the crack.

Feeling real superior about the mature way I had diagnosed the situation, I started to get up off my knees. And in that moment the situation went all to hell again. On the floor, right by my hand were these little pieces of cotton wadding—the same type of wadding I had seen Hamilton pull out of that mattress where Cuba had first hidden the journal.

I started running my hands across the flooring in the back part of the closet. On the right-hand side, about half-way back, I found what I was hunting for: a section of planking in the floor that wobbled.

I worked two of the short, narrow planks out and started feeling around in the space beneath the flooring. First, I felt an old bottle, an old whiskey bottle. Right then I remembered that Miss Maude had told me that her drinking uncle had had the room I was in. Evidently he had kept an emergency bottle stashed in this hole.

Then I felt another bottle. Then I felt something hard and oblong and my scalp started icing up again. I pulled the thing out and it fell open in my hands.

Miss Maude's journal!

CHAPTER THIRTEEN

'd finally found Miss Maude's journal—a black ledger affair—
but instead of congratulating myself I felt like the man who was
so stupid he couldn't find his own rump with both hands.

Hadn't Cuba come into my room the first night the journal
was missing? And hadn't she sneaked into the closet and stayed
there plenty long enough to hide something? Of course, she had
said that she had gone into the closet to get some accessories for
her fancy outfit but that didn't excuse me. Believing *anything*
that girl said was inexcusable.

As to what the other woman in the case, Aunt Elizabeth, had
to do with my finding the journal, I preferred not to think about
it at the time. Just the journal itself had raised enough gooseflesh
on me.

I blew the dust off it, shook out the mattress padding that
had slipped down between the pages and eased back to my chair
by the fire. I was going to have it all digested and put back in its
hiding place before Laura woke up. Then I was going to torture
her with it. Instead, the journal wound up torturing me.

There wasn't a mention of Mary Belle anywhere in it!

The opening entries read like a bird-watcher's journal—just
stuff about the birds Miss Maude had seen migrating through;
the seasons, the weather, etc.

Then things got more personal. In addition to the bird notes
there were references to Hamilton's various guests and the funny
things they said and did. Also there were some amusing little

anecdotes that Miss Maude had told the guests about the ancestral Hamiltons. All very pleasant but where the hell was Mary Belle?

Cuba must have found *something* about her somewhere in all those pages or she wouldn't have taken the risk she had.

I started checking through it again, this time reading the bird notes and all. I still couldn't find a mention of Mary Belle but I did find something else just about as strange. Namely, a recurring reference to a lovebird and a cock-of-the-walk.

What made it strange, for one thing, was that neither bird was native to Spanish Point, as Miss Maude made them out, and for another thing they carried on more like humans than birds. Then it dawned on me. The bird routine—at least part of it—was Miss Maude's way of disguising her more personal items. "Lovebird" could be the code name for Mary Belle and "cock-of-the-walk" could sure as hell represent Hamilton.

I started checking back. The first cryptic reference was an April entry which coincided with the time that Mary Belle had come to Spanish Point:

Another little lovebird arrived. Very pretty but a fledgling. Our cock-of-the-walk much taken with her. Old Buzzard keeping her talons crossed.

"Old Buzzard," I figured was Miss Maude's code name for herself.

A May entry: *Old Buzzard fears lovebird and cock-of-the-walk mating.*

June entry: *Little lovebird wants to mate for life. Her cries getting shriller. Cock-of-the-walk ignoring her fussing.*

July entry: *Old Buzzard fears little lovebird with egg. Mating cry, much shriller.*

That was proof enough for me. I turned to the entry made the day that Mary Belle had disappeared:

Lovebird and cock-of-the-walk have worse fuss yet. My how feathers fly! Old Buzzard in roost hears lovebird shriek. Much relieved to see her fly away with cock-of-the-walk and Flat-Beaked Grouch.

I decoded that to mean that Miss Maude had been up in her room but she could still hear Mary Belle and Hamilton arguing, downstairs maybe. And she had been real relieved to see her ride away with Hamilton and the Flat-Beaked Grouch, meaning Jago.

Then followed three days of entries about the hurricane—this real purple prose about its awesomeness, etc., but nothing about personalities. Then *the* entry, the one made the day after the hurricane had spent itself.

Tragic news. Lovebird drowned in flight to mainland. Cock-of-the-walk so sad but maybe all for best. Old Black Buzzard tells little white lie to Red-Faced Upstart about seeing lovebird fly away but all for best too. Cock-of-the-walk most grateful, poor thing.

Every bit of it fit. The Red-Faced Upstart she had told the little white lie to was Tom Gill, the county chief of police. And naturally Hamilton was grateful.

We finally had him. Or at least we had enough to book him and Jago on suspicion of murder. And as dumb as Jago was, he'd make a slip in his story somewhere along the line and the law would nail them both.

So, I sat there with the journal in my lap, daydreaming and smiling to myself. I could just see Gentleman John Hamilton cringing in the witness chair and the prosecutor quoting those cock-of-the-walk and lovebird entries at him. Then, all of a sudden, the daydream turned into a nightmare.

Standing not five feet away from me and staring right at the journal was Mattie.

She recovered before I did. She gave me this apologetic smile and, in a low voice so as not to awaken Laura, said that she was sorry that she had come in without knocking but she had thought I would be asleep. She had come back for our lunch tray.

That was probably the truth but it didn't alter the fact that she had seen me with a book that was exactly like Miss Maude's journal, and I had looked so guilty that I might as well have been sitting there with Mary Belle's corpse across my lap.

I did the only thing I could do: I smiled and told her it was perfectly all right. I was just going through one of Miss Laura's notebooks.

For an impromptu lie it wasn't bad and Mattie paid me the compliment of acting like she believed me. She got the tray and left. As soon as she did, I jumped to my feet. First, I went over to the closet, put the journal back under the flooring and then closed the door good and tight. Then, I went into Laura's room, got one of her notebooks, came back, sat down again and awaited Hamilton's coming.

About three minutes later, when I was debating whether I should awaken Laura and tell her what had happened, there was a knock on the door. It was so loud that it saved me the trouble of waking Laura up. It was Hamilton.

"Farrell!" he called out.

"Yeah?" I called back in a questioning tone, as though I couldn't imagine why he should come knocking at my door.

"May I come in?"

"Sure," I said, and then motioned to poor, groggy Laura to be quiet.

He came in ... a changed man. He had taken time out from his search for the journal and Cuba to shave, shower and get into some fresh clothes. Now, he was very much the country squire again ... except for one little item. In his right hand was a little black snubnose .38 special.

"Oh, don't be alarmed," he laughed, when he saw Laura and me staring at it. "I'm merely going to clean it and I believe my cleaning kit is in Mr. Farrell's closet."

Laura looked relieved. I probably looked like Simple Simon's big brother. Hamilton switched that leering smile of his from Laura to me.

"With your permission, Mr. Farrell."

What could I say? Mattie, after leaving the room, had evidently waited outside the door and listened. I hadn't given her a thought. All I had been thinking about was hiding the journal again. So she had heard me hustle it over to the closet, hide it, and then close the closet door. Then she had gone down and reported in to Hamilton.

"Permission for what?" I said, stalling for time.

"Why, to enter your closet, of course," he said, smiling even more archly. "It might contain the shirt with the missing button."

"Help yourself," I said. The shirt *was* in the closet but his finger was also around that trigger. If I jumped him or tried to keep him out of the closet there would be a scuffle followed by an unfortunate little "accident" that would leave me with more holes in my head than I already had.

And the worst part of it was this: Laura, in her ignorance of what was transpiring, would believe either that it was an accident or that I had been at fault in attacking Hamilton, when all he wanted to do was go into the closet. I realized then how stupid I had been not to tell her what was going on when I had the chance … but then I had been afraid that *she* might mess things up.

"You are most gracious, Mr. Farrell," Hamilton smirked. "But I assure you it's only the kit I'm after, not the shirt."

He started backing towards the closet, casually making some small talk with Laura enroute. I couldn't bear to look or listen. For a second I thought of locking him in the closet but with my luck he would shoot through the door and put all six slugs in my groin. So I just sat there staring at the floor. I knew that he was actually in the closet when Laura started whispering to me.

"Pete, what's the matter? You look sick."

I nodded in agreement. My only hope was that he couldn't find the journal. Then, in trying to make me tell him where it was, he would get close enough for me to grab the gun. I listened to him in the closet and cringed. He wasn't wasting any time with the shelves, he was exploring the floor. Laura got off the bed, padded across to me in her stocking feet and put her hand to my forehead.

"Pete, sugar, you *are* sick," she said tenderly. "You're all clammy and white as a sheet. Has that s.o.b. done something?"

I nodded again. I could hear Hamilton lifting the flooring. But I couldn't afford to tell Laura what was happening. The way she hated him and with that whiskey still in her she might rush him and that could mean both of us getting killed.

"Pete, say something," she pleaded. "At least open your eyes."

I opened one eye and then closed it real fast. Hamilton was coming out of the closet with an oblong object wrapped in one of the old newspapers he had taken from a shelf.

"Thank you so much, Mr. Farrell," he leered, heading for the door. "I found just what I was hunting for."

He had, too. He'd won. He knew for certain now that the dogs were still on his trail for Mary Belle's murder, but by burning the journal he could stop their baying for good. The only chance we had left was to find Mary Belle's corpse, and in that department the journal hadn't helped a bit.

He slammed the door behind him. I got a good hold on Laura and opened both eyes.

"You know what he had wrapped in that newspaper?"

She blinked.

"You *are* sick. It was just that cleaning kit thing."

"That cleaning kit thing," I sighed, "was Miss Maude's journal. Cuba hid it under the flooring in the closet. I found it while you were asleep. Mattie saw me with it and …"

She took it in just the cool, calm, composed way I had figured she would. She started trying to jerk away from me.

"Don't just sit there, you big idiot. Do something. Tell Miss Maude. It's her book. And it's our whole case."

I tried telling her it wouldn't do any good. Miss Maude probably had intended scratching out the coded references to Mary Belle before giving me the journal. Now, she would be sure to do it. But Laura wouldn't listen. She started hollering.

"Miss Maude! He's got your journal. He's going to …"

I clapped my hand over her mouth and as soon as I did I heard somebody else hollering. It was Jago. He was running up the stairs hollering for Hamilton.

"Mr. John! Mr. John, come on."

Laura and I both rushed out in the hall. Down at the other end of the hall we saw Hamilton come out of his room. Then Jago bounded into view at the top of the stairs. He was in that black rain gear of his and trailing water and mud at every step. He sighted Hamilton but not us.

"Mr. John, the cemetery's washing out!" he bellowed. "The whole damn ocean's come up that creek and they's coffins floating all over the place. We got to …"

As loud as he was bellowing, Hamilton bellowed even louder.

"Stop it! Goddammit, stop that blabbering!"

Jago stopped blabbering, started mumbling to Hamilton instead and they rushed down the stairs together. Laura stared at me.

"Now, what was that all about?"

"The cemetery's washed out," I said, but at the same time feeling the way she did, that there was something more to it than what we had heard. I turned and went back into the room trying to figure the thing out.

"Look," Laura snapped, following me in, "I heard about the cemetery washing out but why should that throw him into such a tizzy?"

I headed for the window. "Maybe he just doesn't want his family tree floating out to sea."

"But, Pete, he didn't sound sad or scared about it. He just sounded ..."

I looked out the window and nodded agreement before she even finished.

"He just sounded mad as hell at Jago for hollering so loud about it."

"That's what I mean," she said, looking out of the window with me. "If my family cemetery was washing away I wouldn't care how loud somebody hollered about it."

She stopped and watched the jeep lights going down the driveway. "He's crazy," she said. "Who's buried there that he doesn't hate? He must be going down to give the coffins a shove."

That's when it came to me. I grabbed Laura, kissed her, and headed for the door. She let out this amazed squawk.

"Pete Farrell, where do you think you're going?"

I didn't answer until I was halfway down the stairs and had a good lead on her.

"To find Mary Belle."

CHAPTER FOURTEEN

grabbed a flashlight and the station wagon keys off the hall table and headed out the back way with Laura still hollering for me to wait. Out in the backyard I almost wished I had waited. It was dark already and the wind had risen from a howl to a shriek and seemed to have everything in it but air: rain, sand, leaves, limbs and at least one garage door—the one to the garage where the station wagon was.

The cemetery, on the banks of the creek, was about a half-mile from the house. Getting to it was like driving through a combination wind tunnel and car wash. Halfway there, I turned off my lights and drove by sound. Every time I ran into something that sounded like wood, I backed up and went around it. Finally, I ran into something that sounded like metal and stopped. It was Hamilton's jeep in the middle of the road.

I grabbed the flashlight and climbed out into the storm and two feet of swirling black water. The wind still shrieked but couldn't drown out the roar of the surf off to my right. It was high tide and since it had run its strongest just as the storm had hit its peak, Hamilton had been brought to grief. The shallow bar at the mouth of the creek had been washed out and the sea had surged in.

I groped my way around the jeep and started sloshing down the flooded road bed towards the creek. The overflow from it worked its way up to my knees, and then I was hip deep in it. It was running a current, ebbing and flowing with the tide.

A log caught me broadside and slowly spun away. A floating tangle of underbrush tripped me. Then I was hit broadside again by what I thought was another log until I started to push it away. It had a handle on it. I grabbed it and switched on the flashlight. I was holding on to a coffin.

I turned the light to the right. Floating in among the trees was another coffin. To the left of it was another. All of the Hamiltons were afloat in their old home-made cypress coffins. I lifted the lid of the one I had and shuddered at the yellow, waxy thing that had once been a man.

I closed the lid, shoved it back into the bushes where I hoped it would hold and waded after the one I had seen in the trees. It had a woman in it. I shoved it aside and started after another floating off in front of me. The water got deeper. I grabbed the coffin and started pulling it back into shallower water. The current started fighting me for it.

I knew why. Straight ahead, maybe forty feet, was the creek channel, where the sea was surging and sucking its strongest. Get too far out in that current and a man was gone. I finally got the coffin under control, viewed its contents, and shoved it back towards shallower water. Then two things happened.

My flashlight fell on a coffin drifting along even further out in the current. I decided against trying for it. But just as I turned chicken I saw two lights shining through the trees down to my right. Hamilton and Jago. They were maybe fifty yards down the creek and doing the same thing I was. I started wading out after the coffin.

I was chest deep in the current before I could grab it. But I couldn't retrieve it. It started pulling *me* with it. Then the Farrell luck changed. The coffin hit a tree and veered towards the shallower side.

I dug in, pulled, got it back into water only hip deep and opened it up. Instead of an ancestral Hamilton, there were the remains of a young blonde girl, a reddish-black mat of blood caked across the front of her white blouse. *Poor little Mary Belle.*

I closed the coffin and started floating it back through the trees towards the car. Suddenly, something smacked the water beside me and whined away. I turned and saw a light coming towards me. It was evidently Hamilton and he was shooting.

I turned off my flashlight, put a tree between me and his light, shoved the coffin up to a couple of saplings and wedged it in between. Then I got behind a big tree about ten feet away. Hamilton kept coming. The beam from his light hit the tree I was behind, then lit up the coffin. There it stayed.

I was lucky. He was thinking more about Mary Belle than he was about me. His light beam stayed on the coffin. The closer he got, the further I worked myself around the other side of the tree. Then he floundered up. Even above the wind I could hear him gasping for breath. He leaned on one of the saplings to rest for a second, straightened up and flashed his light all around, looking for me.

Suddenly, like some sea-going ghoul, he started clawing at the lid of the coffin. When he did I started easing out from behind the tree. By the time he got the lid up I was halfway to him. When he put the light on Mary Belle I sprang.

It was a beautiful spring … but the landing was awful. I had misjudged the distance. Instead of lighting right on top of him like they do in the movies, I fell on my face, right behind him.

But as much as it embarrassed me, it scared him even more. When that splash went up behind him, he let out this helluva yell and dropped his flashlight in the coffin. Then, while I was spluttering to my feet, he got his pistol out of his pocket, fired twice and missed me both times.

Then I hit him. But I'd misjudged it again. Instead of the swing catching him on the jaw, it caught him on the shoulder. He went sprawling backwards over the coffin, lost his pistol enroute, hit on his back in the water and came up right beside a log just the right size to beat the hell out of somebody. Which he proceeded to do to me.

But I kept wading into him. He kept flailing away, backing up and screaming for Jago. Then I felt the current beginning to pull at my legs. He felt it even stronger and tried edging away from it. I kept herding him backwards. The water started coming up over his waist and he changed tactics.

Instead of swinging that driftwood shillelagh sideways, he started swinging it overhand. Fighting in the dark the way we were, it fooled me. The first lick caught me on top of the head and down I went. I came up just in time to hear a scream and a gurgle. He had gone in over his head and the current had him, sucking him out towards the sea. There was one more gurgling scream and then nothing.

I fought my way back to Mary Belle's coffin, guided by the flashlight that Hamilton had dropped inside. I took it out, switched it off, closed the lid on the coffin and started floating the big box through the trees towards the road.

I floundered out onto the road bed about fifty feet below the cars. I headed for them, looking down to the left for signs of Jago. About ten feet from the jeep I found him. The headlights suddenly blazed on, blinding me, and above the wind I heard a voice snarl:

"*Mister* Farrell, I'm about to check yore buttons."

He scared me as much as I had Hamilton. One second I was caught in the light, the next second I plunged into some bushes beside the road and started scrambling for cover. I expected him to start shooting. Instead, the monster showed up in the lights, shoved the coffin in some bushes on the other side of the road and motioned for me to come on out. Instead of shooting me he was going to kill me with his bare hands.

Suddenly, I wasn't tired any more. I got to my feet, made my way through the bushes and sloshed out on the road into the light. He had come out of his rain gear and was standing there with his feet spread apart, his arms tensed; his hands, balled up, looked like a couple of hams with fingers.

"Where's Mr. John?" he hollered.

"With Mary Belle," I hollered back.

He came in swinging. He had a lot of reach on me but he was even wilder than Harney Stokes. I stepped inside his swing, caught him in the mouth and knocked him back across the road.

He got up, spit out some blood and enamel and came at me again; but this time without so much of a rush. I met him half-way, feinted like I was going to hit him low and he swung down at me. I caught him with an overhand right, broke his nose and put him on his back again.

That was all for the Marquis of Queensberry. When he got up this time, he had picked up a stick just a little smaller than a fencepost. I started backing away, tripped, fell and he was on top of me.

First, he held my head under the water and choked me. Just because my tongue shot out about a foot and my eyes started looking like a couple of light bulbs, he got overconfident. He started choking me with one hand and gouging me in the eye with the other. I reached for the gouging hand and got what I wanted. Not the whole hand, just the little finger.

I twisted it back and snapped the bone at the bottom knuckle. The next finger got the same treatment. Suddenly he wasn't choking me. He was just fighting to get that mangled hand free before I peeled back all his fingers. I turned the hand loose, shoved and he went over backwards.

I didn't take advantage of him. I waited for him to get up, knocked him alongside the jeep, pinned him there and went to work on him. I hit him once for Mary Belle, once for Cuba, and then I really let him have it.

"This one, you bastard, is for knocking on my door this morning!"

He fell and hit the water on what was left of his face. I could have let him drown right there but I was nice to him. I got some rope out of the jeep, tied him up and draped him over the hood of the station wagon. Then I put the back seats down, lowered the tailgate and slid Mary Belle's coffin inside.

Thinking everything was all over, I was just about to get in the car myself when I saw *another* light coming towards me—this time from the direction of the house.

I couldn't help groaning. Would I have to fight Mattie, *too?* Or was it Laura? The light looked like it was maybe a hundred yards away and coming slow. I decided to try Jago's trick. I made sure he was secured to the hood, got in, and somehow got the car backed around and pointed down the road towards the light.

It kept coming. When it was about thirty yards off, I ducked low enough so that if it was Mattie, Jago would catch the bullet instead of me. Then I turned on the headlights. A split second later the windshield shattered and a slug ripped through the roof. It *was* Mattie.

I opened the door on the far side and slid out into the water on my face just as another slug hit the windshield. Once I got into the bushes, I raised up and took a look. As I did, a third slug hit the car. Then I was on my feet hollering.

"For God's sake, Laura! Put that thing down!"

Even with all the wind, she heard me. Hamilton's "sweet" little old deer rifle splashed into the water at her feet.

"Pete!"

Then she was in my arms sobbing. She was so sure they had killed me that she had come to kill them.

I told her about Hamilton drowning. I told her that Jago was draped over the hood. She sobbed some more. Then I told her about Mary Belle.

"Hamilton figured he could bury her in a place safer than the sea. He buried her in somebody else's coffin."

That did it.

She stopped sobbing, drew away, and looked up at me accusingly.

"It was Aunt Elizabeth's coffin he put Mary Belle in, wasn't it? And he just dumped Aunt Elizabeth in the bottom of the grave probably. That's why she was walking. And don't laugh, Pete Farrell, it's the truth!"

I'd known all along she was going to think that.

EPILOGUE

Well, Laura and I are married now and working as a team. The matter of who's captain of the team hasn't been decided yet, despite what Laura says. Seeing as how I fell from grace and temporarily became a writer myself, I couldn't get out of marrying her.

We've got a big, new home back in my home town of Stanton that we paid for with the money we got from one Ben Ponza for a certain story and pictures. His screams, when we named our price, constituted the sweetest music I ever heard.

Miss Maude has recovered from the shock and is now operating Oakhurst and the island as a resort for honeymooners. All her guests love the place, especially since they don't encounter the same amatory hazards as I did.

Jago is in the penitentiary and will be for quite a spell. Not, however, for being an accomplice to murder. He revealed in court that technically John Hamilton did not murder Mary Belle. It came about when they were having that violent argument in the library, the one Miss Maude had overheard.

Mary Belle was demanding that Hamilton marry her because she was pregnant. When he gave her a final no, suggesting that she go away instead, Mary Belle became enraged, grabbed the big, old, seaman's knife from the wall over his desk and tried to kill him. They struggled, fell to the floor and the knife pierced her chest.

Hamilton evidently realized what the bad publicity would do to his precious career and what a helluva time he would have proving his innocence with Mary Belle being pregnant. So, he decided just to dispose of the body and blame it on the hurricane.

Jago brought the car around front, out of view of Miss Maude's window. When they had Mary Belle propped between them, they moved out into the driveway in view of Miss Maude. Hamilton then called up to her about something, saw that she got an angle view of Mary Belle and then they took off.

Hamilton was helped by the fact that Miss Maude was on one of her binges and had been boozing in her room for a couple of days. By the time she came down, Mattie had all traces of the accident removed.

Jago also revealed in court that he wanted to dump the body at sea but Hamilton said he knew an even safer place. The last place anybody would look would be in somebody else's grave. He got a fiendish pleasure out of putting her in the cemetery with his high and mighty ancestors.

Three days of rain removed all trace of their work. As to whose grave and coffin she was put in, Jago claimed that he couldn't remember. And it's a damn good thing he couldn't. If he had said Aunt Elizabeth's grave I would have hanged him personally. He also confessed that I was right about their attempt to do away with Cuba.

As for good old Cuba, I found out she was even more of a fiendish liar than I suspected. Not only was she working for the police, she was also working for Ben Ponza. When I found that out, Laura and I tacked an extra ten thousand on the price we charged him for the pictures and stories. Laura hadn't had the slightest idea that Cuba was working for Ben either.

It seemed that Ben had been courting her in New York and she was giving him the torture treatment, too. Then the day that

Mary Belle was discovered missing, Ben received a call from Tom Gill, whom he had met on various trips to Spanish Point and Queensport.

Tom, remembering that Ben had seen Hamilton and Mary Belle together on the island, wondered if Hamilton had ever said anything to him about their relationship. He was the type who would brag about such things. Ben wound up getting the rest of the story out of Tom. And, remembering the lousy trick that Hamilton had played on him, he pledged Gill his all-out support.

Knowing that Hamilton would be needing a new secretary, he suggested a type that could keep Hamilton enthralled and, if she couldn't get anything out of him, get it from Miss Maude. He told Tom that he knew just the girl for the job—Miss Cuba Paxton.

At first, Cuba didn't want any part of the job, but Ben was thirsting so for revenge that he promised to take her on a deluxe 'round-the-world tour when the job was over. Cuba agreed. Ben knew that Hamilton had a lecture on tap in Baltimore and that there would be a cocktail party in his honor. He got Cuba invited to the party and the rest was simple.

Her second week on the island, Cuba discovered that Miss Maude was keeping a journal, sneaked a look at it, and realized how damaging the little "bird" stories could be.

Plans then called for Cuba to stick around another month and find out more about Miss Maude's activities the day of the tragedy and thus wreck her alibi for Hamilton.

Ben, realizing that he might really be able to hang Hamilton, threw in his reserves, namely, me and Laura ... without telling Laura anything about Cuba. We would get pictures, background stuff, etc., and when we left the island, Cuba and the journal would leave with us. In case anything went wrong, I would be there to handle it.

But Cuba couldn't wait. That drunken afternoon when she heard Miss Maude telling me about the journal, she was afraid that I would realize its potential and beat her to stealing it.

So she went up, got it and hid it in her mattress ... hoping that Miss Maude, what with having guests and being about to go on another jag, wouldn't miss it until we were gone. And she was also scared that if I got the journal, Ben might renege on his promise of the 'round- the-world cruise.

But as Miss Maude got drunker and tried to show me the journal, everything went to hell—especially when Hamilton realized the danger it represented. So, after he had Jago search Cuba's room and I told her about it, she transferred the journal to my closet and made plans to flee the island. Her plan the next morning was to ride innocently down to the dock, take the boat and report in to Tom Gill in Queensport.

Tom would provide her with a husky "boy friend" to take her back to the island. There, on the pretense of being fed up with Hamilton, she would pack her clothes and the journal and leave the island.

The "boy friend," she would claim, was a cutie she had picked up on one of her Saturday trips into Queensport. That way neither Laura nor I could have any claim whatsoever to having helped crack the case, and Cuba and Ben would head around the world.

And they did go around the world and both of the heartless fiends got just what they deserved. The first night on board ship, Cuba taunted Ben so with her charms, ran him so crazy, that he routed the captain out and he married them.

God, how they deserved one another. Every time Laura and I visit them, Ben spends most of his time trying to figure out those mysterious smiles I get from Cuba. And I don't do a damn thing to keep him from thinking the worst.

As for the ghosts … did Laura really see Aunt Elizabeth? Did Aunt Elizabeth lead me to the journal? I refuse to answer on the grounds that it might incriminate me. In short, every time I say anything on the subject, Laura makes me sleep on top of the cover!

THE END

www.ingramcontent.com/pod-product-compliance
Lightning Source LLC
Chambersburg PA
CBHW030128260626
47156CB00008B/2853